An Unlikely LOVE STORY

Ellie Hall

ABOUT THIS BOOK

Falling in love is against Hazel's rules. Maxwell doesn't care about rules, rather recipes. But will he whip one up for a happily ever after?

My full name is Hazel Loves, yes really, but I have no interest in relationships. In fact, I live by three rules:

1. Never meet the pets, parents, or best friend.
2. Never date the same guy twice.
3. Never fall in love.

That's a lot of nevers. I thought I was a rebel and not above breaking rules until I broke my own.

A vanilla latte with a heart in the foam formed a crack in my exterior. Then the batch of chocolate chip cookies softened something inside. Never mind, scratch that, it was Maxwell—my neighbor.

As I struggle with being strong, single, and on the scene and the mushy, melty, romantic within, I try desperately not to fall in love. But what's wrong with falling if you have someone with dark tousled hair, refined yet ruggedly handsome features, and chiseled arms to catch you?

Nothing. Nothing at all.

Scratch that. Everything.

CHAPTER 1
BAKE BABY BAKE
MAXWELL

I scrape the last bits from the edge of the bowl. I lick the spoon. I glimpse a warped reflection of myself in the stainless steel refrigerator door and stop short.

I've licked clean the bowl of cookie dough. Who am I?

What happened to Maxwell, who dated a new girl every weekend? The BMW. The trips. The freedom. The guy who could go wherever he wanted, whenever he wanted... Well, I can still do all the above but not without thinking about *her*.

I was insatiable. I always wanted more. Now I just want *her*.

Nights in.

Nights out.

Days and days, a lifetime with Hazel.

The timer beeps. This time I catch my reflection in the double oven doors. My muddled thoughts do not erase the fact that I'm wearing a red apron that says *Kiss the Cook*. (Underneath, I have a fitted white T-shirt with a buttery smear on the sleeve. Let's just say I'm not the most careful baker.) My muscles still pop under the bronzed evidence of my trip to St. Tropez last month, but I have a coordinating red oven mitt on my hand to check on the sheet of chocolate chip cookies in the oven.

Are you confused? Yeah, me too.

Last Saturday night I was at Javier's. It's a private lounge with leather and dark wood. Captains of industry and cards. Moody lighting and guys like me—Ivy League grads who aren't total jerks. Well, some of us are, but we look good doing it. It's where we go instead of sweaty clubs with gold-diggers. It's elite and so is the rest of the clientele, men and women alike. The latter are educated, take care of themselves because they can afford to, and share the understanding that work and whatever other hang-ups we have about relationships mean we're there for a no-strings kind of arrangement and nothing more.

I met a gal who has her MFA and was in the Top 30 Under 30 this year. She crushes lesser men—and women—under her stilettos. She can talk her way through an executive meeting and leave the room thunderstruck. After our dinner date, she didn't call or text the next day or the day after that or at all this week.

That's how I liked it. An evening at Javier's, conversation over a good meal, and then do it all over again the next weekend. It was a neat and tidy arrangement.

I check my phone. No new messages. Until recently, I didn't worry about wants and needs, relationships, and trips to home goods stores like Bed, Bath, and Beyond.

Now, here I am *beyond*. Just absolutely beyond.

Call me a jerk for going to Javier's last weekend. Yes, I like Hazel. Maybe more than like, but I'm not sure I'm ready to go there—to become someone else... Who? Who would I be if we started dating? If we became a couple? If we...fell in love?

Whoa, there buddy.

I'm not superstitious, but maybe Hazel Loves bewitched me that first time we met. She and her roommate Catherine had just moved in down the hall. Hazel came parading out of their apartment—hot as a summer day, even though it's winter, and as sweet as can be—and introduced herself. Hazel talked about her wedding...

Blam! I pictured her in a white gown. It was fitted and silky—a thin layer caressing her curves. Her hair cascaded over her shoulders and she smiled at me—a strange and lovely and bewitching smile. Then I saw myself at the other end of the aisle in a tux. Halloween costumes? It was January. No such luck.

Guys, I visualized us getting married. Do you know what that means? The beginning of the end.

The image stayed with me all morning, through a meeting with corporate—I had to get notes from Conrad because I didn't absorb a blasted thing from the presentation. Then at lunch, I ordered a chicken salad and I swear I was considering catering options, appetizers, cakes—three course meal or buffet style?

What does this mean?

The brief conversation with Hazel about weddings trailed me for the rest of the week and even during the weird yoga-date as part of a dare with her roommate. But it wasn't really a date because Hazel was there too. Catherine had her eye on the burly, military guy she was talking to when I met them at the studio. All I could think about during the sweat session was Hazel on the yoga mat by my side.

Have I ever been self-conscious a day in my life? No. Call me blessed. Whatever. But that day? The teacher wanted me to put my knee where? Extend my arm along my side-what? It was all I could do not to fall on my backside.

Before, during, and afterward, it was Hazel, Hazel, Hazel. All I can do to stop myself from knocking on her apartment door down the hall is...yup, you got it. Baking. Why?

Was my mother a proficient baker? Nope.

Did I excel in home economics? No chance.

Do I have a sweet tooth? Not really.

I'd gathered that Hazel likes baked goods, well, when Catherine bakes and so...yeah. You get it. But I don't. That's a problem. This has never happened to me before. I just have to make sure I don't make a complete fool of myself. When have I ever cared about that? Never because it's never been an issue. Who am I?

The worst of it though is that every time I see another

woman, I see Hazel's face. I long for her hands in mine, strolling through the park, ducking into a cozy coffee shop, watching a movie with our feet touching.

Really, Maxwell?

I toss the spoon in the sink with a clang. I picture spooning Hazel in my arms. I've never spooned a woman. Well, once. One woman. Never again. I learned my lesson.

I dream about meals together. Breakfast, lunch, dinner. Trips to exotic locales, holidays, birthdays... I see her in my future and it's all I want.

After cleaning up, I try to distract myself with earnings reports and fiduciary lending. I can't concentrate. Is this what happens when you fall?

So, what have I done when day after day I can't get her out of my mind? I make cookies...with her in mind. But it hasn't stopped there. I've made brownies, breads, cakes...then moved on to pastries, torts, and tarts.

I have become Betty Crocker, only my name is Maxwell Davis and I'm a multi-millionaire. Come to think of it, Betty probably was too when all was said and done.

Don't you dare tell a soul.

The cookies are Hazel's roommate's recipe. Or her grandmother's. I forget. Secret ingredient? Cream cheese. Before that, did I have any idea how to combine sugar and butter to make something edible? Not even a clue.

But now I know the timing and temperature required to achieve the perfect bake.

How did I acquire that recipe? Catherine was out of sugar. Needed to borrow some. I had a few packets for when guests came for coffee, a rarity. We started chatting, and she explained she was making the cookies because of the coming storm. Sounds cozy, right?

Then she off-handedly mentioned they're Hazel's favorite.

Have you ever had that moment when everything around

you goes quiet and you zone in on something? I imagine it's what happens to a dog when it catches a scent.

Am I a dog? Probably.

But Catherine's comment lit something in me, and I've been baking ever since. I probably shouldn't admit all of this. But it's too late. I've been bringing all my baked items into the office. My assistant, colleagues, and clients are starting to give me strange looks.

Before this, I'd never baked a cookie in my life—well, once, but it was a disaster and my sister says it doesn't count. Until recently, I never even turned on the oven in my kitchen since moving in over a year ago. The real estate agent told me it was a Viking, had all the bells and whistles, blah, blah, blah. It didn't matter because I had no plans on using it. It was new and stainless steel and that was good enough for me.

Now the buttery, sweet scent of chocolate wafts out and if I had Hazel in here with me, I'd be in heaven.

But I'm getting ahead of myself. Here's what happened: I saw Hazel that first day and it was instant chemistry, like when baking powder and water combine, releasing carbon dioxide into a batter. It's an acid-base reaction, prompting bubbles to form, expand, and leaven the mixture.

Have I been leavened? Yeah. I think I'm in leaven. I mean...never mind.

Hazel didn't have a ring on her finger when she was talking about her wedding plans, so I thought maybe she was theorizing and the fiancé was hypothetical.

Wishful thinking on my part?

I was in luck. The good news: she wasn't engaged. The bad news: she's hardly home.

Likely, she has a boyfriend or suitors at least.

When I step foot into the hall, I sometimes catch a hit of Hazel's vanilla, citrus scent. But rarely do I see her. I can't forget about her voice—she has a lovely British accent that's both soothing and confident. It's the kind of voice you'd want by your bedside if you were diagnosed with a disease or a broken limb. The kind of voice that would assure you everything would be okay.

The sensory experience of Hazel makes the world go fuzzy, and I become a blithering schoolboy with his first crush and not a stud. Yeah, I've been called that on multiple occasions. Does that make me sound like an arrogant jerk?

I'm working on it because what it turns out I want most in my life isn't for jerks—or the faint of heart.

Back to the recipe. The first batch was a burned disaster.

On the second try, I forgot the salt—believe it or not, it enhances the flavor of the chocolate—I only know that because I read it in a magazine during a flight...and then again during hours of internet research to try to understand baking chemistry.

Refrain from the eye roll, please.

The third time was a success and I've been testing batches for consistency and to make sure it wasn't a fluke.

Those cookies and that woman changed me.

Did she ruin me? Maybe, but I can't say I'm sorry.

She planted a seed. Something new grows within.

And now I bake cookies like it's my hobby.

My heart stutters at the thought of her in my arms. My lips on hers. The vision of her walking down the aisle toward me.

Let me paint a picture: she's graceful—goes on for miles and miles. Those legs. There should be a speed limit or some kind of traffic law. Sound the sirens, slow me down. But I can't, I won't.

She's tall, but a few inches shorter than me. Her hair is the mane of a lioness. Her eyes spark with light and intelligence. And that's the thing. I want to hear her talk. Before you judge me, I'm not a jerk who thinks women are all looks and no substance. Nothing of the sort.

Remember Javier's? I forget exactly, but I think you have to take an IQ test to get through the doors. Hazel would pass with flying colors. Aside from her having her Ph.D. and speaking intelligently on all manner of topics, I want to hear her talk about herself, her life, her goals and hopes and dreams. There's so much to her it's distracting, making me forget things like my dry cleaning. I was picturing her coming up over the hill during a round of golf during a quick business trip to Florida. I missed a swing I've never missed before.

At inopportune and completely random moments, I find myself contemplating Hazel with absolute wonder.

If you know me, which you're only just getting to, that's unusual, to say the least. No, not unusual, ten kinds of crazy. This is why I'm worried I've gone mad or she's used some kind of witchery on me. I'm the guy who doesn't plan to settle down. Who likes the freedom of my jet-setting life.

Have I ever considered getting a dog or a cat? Probably not.

Kids? Nope. A dad who's always away on business probably isn't a good thing.

A partner to make decisions with about the future and table arrangements? Not until Hazel.

I scrub my oven-mitted hand down my face. I hardly know myself anymore. However, I do know that I feel something for this woman that I never expected. Not in a million years. I went from a guy who could have any woman I wanted to only desiring one. I'll do anything to convince her I'm worthy.

But I'm going to spend the next fifteen minutes talking myself out of going next door with my latest batch of fresh from the oven cookies.

Watch me fail...fall. Well, whatever. Probably both.

CHAPTER 2
GALENTINE'S DAY
HAZEL

I eat when I'm happy. I eat when I'm in good company. I eat when I'm in...love? Nope. Never. Not this girl. Not in love. Not ever.

I eat when I think about Maxwell. No. No. No. Why is the guy in 7G taking up so much real estate in my mind? That's rent free, prime property, people! And yet he's moved in, unpacked, and settled down.

Oh, dear.

I help myself to a handful of popcorn confetti-ed with those chalky but irresistible Conversation Hearts that come out every year around Valentine's Day. I read one before I pop it into my mouth. The faint print says *Call me.*

Call who? Maxwell? No. I don't call guys unless I need something painted, fixed, hung, or replaced, and that's rare. I'm a do-it-yourself kind of gal. Give me a hammer, wrench, and a how-to video. Then consider the job done.

I only call a guy to go on a date if I'm certain he understands my particular situation. As in, I don't want one. Not a short term, long term, or any kind of commitment. No strings. No attachments. Nothing that later requires tissues, a tub of ice cream, and a Netflix binge.

I don't get my heart broken because I don't get involved for longer than a date. On the other hand, I've broken a few hearts and I'm not proud. It's easier to keep emotions out of the deal from the beginning.

No, I won't call Maxwell. I won't press the button beneath his photo on my phone. I won't.

Before you get carried away thinking I'm contradicting myself, just know that he put the photo and his number there. I glance at the image now: tousled dark hair and refined yet ruggedly handsome features, a thin shadow of scruff along his jawline, leading to a tease of tanned skin from his V-neck shirt.

We're neighbors and early one morning, as the sun came up, gilding the city silver and sparkly, we were leaving the building at the same time. I was heading out to an early morning yoga class, and he was leaving for work. He snagged my phone, snapped a photo, and entered his number. No comment. That was it.

No lame pick up line. No awkward conversation. Straight and to the point.

No strings. No attachments. Just how I like it.

Only, it's like a string leads me to him, wraps around him, attaches my every thought to him.

I refuse to think about him except that I am. I'm constantly thinking about his full head of hair, the scratch of stubble along his jaw, and those eyes.

A little whimper escapes.

"Hazel, are you okay?" Colette asks, pulling me from my punch-drunk stupor.

I down the rest of my pink lemonade. "I'm just fine, dandy, exemplary, peachy—" I put my hand over my face. What am I saying? Who talks like that? Someone who's losing her mind, that's who.

Colette gives me a long side-eye. "Who's that?" Her finger aims for the image on my phone before it fades to a blank screen.

"No one."

"No One. Is that his full name? Well, he's hot," Lottie says, popping between our shoulders.

"You didn't see him," I reply.

"Didn't have to. Every guy you've ever dated is, how shall I put it? Very kind on the eyes."

"Ladies," an ordinarily gentle voice booms in our direction.

The three of us jitter and turn around. Minnie faces us with one hand on her hip. In the other, she holds a platter of cinnamon rolls slathered in gooey frosting and with a light dusting of red and purple Valentine's sprinkles.

"Ooh, they're made into the shape of hearts," Colette says, diffusing the tension.

"And they smell delicious," I add.

"Girls, this is a *Gal*entine's Day party. No talking about guys."

"Oh yeah, that's right. No boys allowed," Lottie says disappointedly.

"What about me?" a deep, male voice says.

We all spin in the direction of the doorway.

"What? I'm your honorary babe," Tyler says. With his arms full, he gently kicks the door closed behind him. "You can't turn me away because I come bearing gifts." He has a pastry box in one arm. He passes an outrageous bouquet of flowers to Minnie and then produces some chocolate. "Direct from France."

Huh. We're all best friends, but the slight blush of rose matching the flowers in Minnie's arms suggests something. I'll have to investigate later. Right now, I'm wondering who the traitor is. "Who invited the guy to our Galentine's Day brunch?" I demand.

Minnie goes a shade darker.

"Our honorary babe?" Lottie harrumphs. "Who happens to be the most handsome male specimen any of us have ever laid eyes on. I still say it's a shame you're like Hazel and refuse to settle down."

"Oh, like any of you are looking to tie-the-knot soon," Tyler says pointedly.

"'Ovaries before broveries,'" Collette and Lottie say in unison, quoting the television show *Parks and Recreation*.

"I miss those days," Minnie says.

We all nod in agreement. If this were a TV show, the music and lighting would soften, the camera would pan to each of us looking reflective, and then transition to a montage during college when we'd all get together each week to watch a new episode. This is also the source of the Galentine's Day festivities at present.

Tyler lands a kiss on each of our cheeks, in quite the European way, having recently traveled there for one of his epic expeditions. I didn't think it was possible, but Minnie's cheeks go darker and now resemble the corny heart decorations we strung up.

He juts his chin at the banner over the serving table at my back. "Happy Galentine's Day," he reads. "And here I thought it was a welcome home soiree."

"Welcome home," I say. "How was Hossegor?"

"The surf was firing. Then I went to Paris." He sighs. "I'll tell you all about it, but first, you have to try these strawberry éclairs and apple rose tartlets and lavender madeleines, and—"

We all dip into the box before he even has a chance to set it down.

"Any stories of *amour* from France?" Colette asks, coming from the kitchen with a fresh pitcher of the homemade pink lemonade.

Tyler takes a generous bite of an éclair and waggles his eyebrows.

"This is why it was supposed to be a *no boys allowed* function," Minnie mutters.

He bites his lip. "Since I only heard about this party now, please explain why you're all wearing your pajamas—adorable by the way," he says to Minnie, gesturing to the shorts with little hearts and Minnie Mouse heads.

I'm wearing a set with heart-shaped cat paw prints.

"Because comfort is our top priority and these are Mew approved," I say when my cat slinks by. I give him a pet.

"No exceptions to Galentine's Day, huh?" Tyler asks, motioning to the banner. "I've never really understood what it is, but—"

With impeccable timing, from the living room television, Leslie's voice (of *Parks and Recreation* fame), explains. "Oh, it's only the best day of the year. Every February thirteenth, my lady friends and I leave our husbands and our boyfriends at home, and we just come and kick it, breakfast-style. Ladies celebrating ladies. It's like Lilith Fair, minus the angst. Plus frittatas."

The six of us ladies recite the lines from the show verbatim.

"It's become a tradition to play past episodes of the show, brunch, gab, and chill," Colette says.

"But no boys," I say, my mind landing on one very specific boy...er, man.

"And manis, pedis, chocolate..." Minnie adds, outlining our plans for the rest of the morning.

"But someone is missing." Tyler turns in a circle, then his eyes widen with alarm. "Where is Catherine?"

"She abandoned us," Minnie says with a sigh.

"High tailed it out of here," Colette adds.

"Left on a jet plane," Lottie says.

"She fell in love," I answer.

"Traitor," Tyler says.

"Traditionally, we celebrate Galentine's Day on February thirteen, but Minnie was out of town for work, so we had to postpone until a few days later," I explain. "Then Catherine had to leave for romantic Rome. Plus, I'm all for celebrating my friendships anytime."

"So you were talking about frittatas?" Tyler says. "What can I help with?"

Apparently, he's staying.

"Everything is ready. All you have to do is sit your sweet, imposter buns down," Colette says in her slight southern accent.

"So you're not kicking me out?" he asks.

I risk a glance at Minnie. She suddenly finds the wood floor fascinating.

I lead everyone into the dining room. Yes, we're in Manhattan and yes, there is a dining room. A proper one with a chandelier.

Before you go thinking that my friends and me are beautiful and rich—well, we are—our respective wealth was earned, hard-won, or in Minnie's case, inherited. Her parents tragically died in a freak accident off the coast of Australia where they were studying a rare—well, I can't remember what, but it was some kind of prickly, deadly fish. She was just a kid and sent to live with her aunt. She's since passed on, leaving Minnie without family, but with a very, very nice piece of prime real estate overlooking Central Park. Would she trade it to have more time with the people she loves? Absolutely. But since that's not possible, she welcomes those of us she cares most about into her home as often as possible, which is a real treat because I feel like a Disney princess when in her not-so-humble abode.

But I digress... We were supposed to be at Minnie's today. However, as mentioned, she was away for work, so I raised my hand and offered to host brunch. Also, her neighbor is a grouch. Anyway, the apartment I share with Catherine isn't too shabby, if I do say so myself.

We gather around the table, festooned in red, purple, and gold: flowers, streamers, banners, pom-poms, confetti, balloons, and platters and trays and plates piled with food.

"Food glorious food!" I sing.

"It's like the entire Valentine's Day décor section at Target exploded in here!" Lottie exclaims.

"Well, I love you girls. And you too, Tyler," I say with a smile.

"And we love your enthusiasm," he says. His gaze lingers on Minnie for a long beat, then he adds, "Thanks for letting me stay."

Tyler's mother is in France and I've never heard him discuss his father. Despite bi-annual visits to surf and visit his mom, we're his stateside fam.

We dig into waffles with strawberries, pancakes with blueberries, quiche, scones, and frittata, of course.

"This is delicious," Colette says.

"Scrummy," Lottie adds.

"I'm so glad I happened by," Tyler says around a mouthful.

"I want to offer a toast," I say, getting to my feet. "Roses are red, violets are blue, you girls—and Tyler—are my best friends, and I don't know what I'd do without you."

There's a round of *aws* and the clinking of our glasses followed by variations on the last part of the rhyme, descending into silly jokes and a debate about whether violets are blue or purple. I just roll with the laughter—it's good for the heart and soul. Especially when that heart sometimes feels a little bit lonely despite being surrounded by so much love.

Minnie pulls us from the hysterics and suggests we play a game. "It's really easy." She passes out pink cards printed with the beginnings of sentences. "It's kind of like truth or dare, but just with the truth part. Going around the table, all we have to do is finish the sentences. However, there's one catch." She holds up a bowl filled with crumpled paper. "If you draw the letter *G* you have to answer it from a *Galentine* point of view so anything goes. If you draw a *V*, it's all about the *Valentine*—true romance. Got it? I'll go first so you can see how it works."

I glance down at the sentence on my card and fold it up, hoping I get *G*.

Minnie reads from her card. "My heart beats for ____." She draws the letter *G*.

"The truth is my heart beats for Gilmore Girls reruns."

There's a chorus of approval.

Colette goes next. "The sweetest thing ____ has ever done for me is _____." She pulls a folded paper from the bowl and says, "V. Easy. The sweetest thing my high school sweetheart ever did for me was win me a giant jar of chocolate kisses at the sweetheart dance." She coos then smirks.

I arch an eyebrow in question.

"He guessed how many were in the jar. Then he gave me that many kisses."

"So romantic," Minnie says.

I glance at my card again and pray for the letter G. *Galentine, Galentine, Galentine.*

"Hazel's turn," Minnie says, keeping the game moving while I serve seconds of the frittata. I take a painstakingly long time to chew. I hoped that a couple of conversations would strike up, taking attention off the game. No such luck.

"Ok. My sentence is: When I think about ______ I get all mushy inside." Since this is a game of truth and I'd never lie to you, I have to admit that my voice shakes a little bit.

All eyes are on me. Every single one. Surrounded by all the red and purple, hearts and confetti, it's intense. I draw from the bowl of crumpled paper. *G, please.*

"Hazel got V for Valentine," Tyler says, smirking as if he knows something I am certain he doesn't. Whatever wacky thing is going on in my mind when it comes to the guy next door, it's a secret. One I will take to the grave.

Colette rolls her wrist, motioning for me to get on with it already.

I clear my throat.

They lean in.

Then, someone knocks on the door.

We all startle.

I bounce from my seat. "I'll get it." My letter V for Valentine flies across the table.

They give me variations on puzzled looks. Of course, I'll get it. This is my house. But they didn't miss my jittery display of nerves. Nope, you can't get anything past a group of best friends.

I have no doubt they're wondering and whispering about why I hesitated.

Taking a deep breath, I smooth my hair as I reach for the doorknob and pull it open.

Remember when I described a guy with tousled dark hair and refined yet ruggedly handsome features? The one with a thin shadow of scruff along his jawline? He's also impossibly fit, confident, tall, and standing in my doorway.

My heart pirouettes. My stomach does a relevé.

Maxwell smirks, looking me up and down. "Cute."

"Meow?" I say. Why did I think pajamas with cat paw hearts were a good idea?

CHAPTER 3
CHOCOLATE CHIP SUPER HERO
MAXWELL

I'm not the kind of guy to gaze at the floor, my hands, or make someone suffer in awkward silence.

What kind of guy am I? The one from an obnoxious—or enviable, depending on who you ask—luxury car, watch, or cologne commercial.

Obnoxious because I don't, in fact, have an inner monologue when I'm driving at high speeds down a rain-streaked street. Nor do I admire my watch, so it catches the light just so. Never have I ever walked through an empty European plaza while a random and beautiful woman walked toward me before falling into my embrace. Okay, there was that one time in Berlin.

For better or worse, I have tall, dark, handsome, and powerful dialed in. I don't say that to sound arrogant. Rather, it's a business advantage. The same way I worked my way to closing multi-million dollar deals with everyone coming out of the boardroom feeling like they've won, I also had to learn how to command a room, ensure that people trust that I know what I'm doing, and look the part.

Mission accomplished when I speak clearly, concisely, and confidently.

Mission failed when I'm standing here in the hall, gobsmacked and holding a platter of chocolate chip cookies.

Hazel is the first to crack. She bites her lip. Why does she have to draw attention to her lips?

Why? Oh, right, because they're perfect along with everything else about her. I'm ruined. Ruined forever by this gorgeous woman.

"You, uh, have something—" She extends her hand and brushes my cheek gently.

I force myself not to lean into her touch.

What have I become?

"A crumb?" she asks, gesturing to the cookies.

The corner of my lip lifts effortlessly. "I had to taste test."

Laughter comes from behind me.

"Oh, I didn't realize you had company."

"We, uh," she stutters. She shifts from foot to foot.

My eyes narrow and realization triggers a little burst of soft light inside of me. Are we having the same effect on each other?

A tall guy emerges from down the hall.

The light within goes dark. I was wrong. Very wrong. Hazel has a boyfriend. Strange though, the dude could be my doppelganger. Maybe she has a type?

We size each other up for a long moment. He looks oddly familiar, but I am certain we've never met.

He points at himself. "Token dude at the girlfest. I'd be way more comfortable if there were two of us. I'm Tyler by the way."

Confusion takes hold and my brow furrows, but I have the presence of mind to introduce myself. "Nice to meet you. I'm Maxwell Davis."

Hazel's eyes widen.

Female laughter echoes from down the hall. Relief sweeps through me. They're not alone.

"He crashed my Galentine's Day party," Hazel says in her British accent.

Tyler pokes Hazel's arm like an overgrown child. "Come on, say yes, Mom. He brought cookies." He's hardly taken his eye off the plate.

"I thought you had a thing for pastries."

He shrugs. "*French* pastries. Despite my mother's origins, I'm all American. Come on, Chocolate Chip," he says to me. "You're my new hero."

The guy hip checks Hazel, presses past her, and takes the cookies from my hands. "If I'm the honorary babe. That makes you, resident darling." I catch Tyler toss a wink in Hazel's direction.

I follow them down the hall, catching her vanilla-citrus scent under an assortment of brunch foods. Regretfully, I'm unable to ignore the way she looks in those cute shorts with the heart-shaped paw prints.

The room goes quiet when we enter. A small woman with dark hair squeaks.

I eye Hazel and she seems to shrink.

"Everyone, meet Maxwell. Maxwell, meet everyone." She then goes on to introduce me to Lottie, Colette, and the dark-haired woman, Minnie.

"You guys look so much alike," she says, shaking her head slowly and looking from Tyler to me. "Odd."

Tyler and I look at each other. We're both tall, have dark hair, and are fit.

"His nose is different. Eyes too," Hazel says softly. "Also, Tyler and I go way back." She shakes her head as if dismissing a thought.

I pull myself together, and say, "I see you have quite the spread already, but I brought cookies."

Tyler sets them on the table.

"Those are Catherine's grandmother's recipe, aren't they?" Hazel says, diving for one.

As if shaking themselves out of a collective stupor at the

introduction of another guy at a gal's party, everyone helps themselves and conversation resumes.

I take a seat to Hazel's right and she passes me a plate.

"No one is allowed to leave until they join the clean plate club," Colette says with a wink.

"We were playing a game. It was Hazel's turn." Lottie holds up a slip of paper.

They all go quiet and stare at Hazel.

She stuffs the rest of the cookie in her mouth. After a long moment, she clears her throat, and says, "When I think about Catherine, I get all—"

"We know you miss her, but that paper says *V*, honey," Colette exclaims. Then to me she adds, "It's like truth or dare, but the dare is you have to answer according to your romantic life or your gal-pal life depending on whether you draw a *V* for Valentine or a *G* for Galentine."

"When I think about, um, this guy I, get—" Hazel breaks off again.

"What guy?" Lottie fires from across the table.

"Who?" Minnie asks. "Don't tell me it's that guy we met last month." She frowns.

Lottie reads over Hazel's shoulder, "When I think about, blank, I get all mushy inside. Who makes you mushy, Hazel? Huh? Huh?" She elbows her friend.

Hazel shakes her head.

Colette hops to her feet and swoops a cell phone out of a basket sitting on a table along the wall. They must have a no cell-phones while eating rule.

She clicks it on.

Lightning fast, Hazel launches to her feet, grabbing for it.

But it's too late. The screen opens to a contact page with a number and photograph at the top. It's far away, but I glimpse it before Hazel nabs her phone back.

"Hazel Loves, what are you keeping from us?" Tyler asks, sparing me a glance.

Minnie points at Hazel. "I know that look. I know it well. Our girl Hazel is smitten."

"Oh yeah, how do you know that look so well, Miss Minnie? Huh? Huh?" Hazel asks accusingly, catting her eyes between Minnie and Tyler.

Minnie goes still.

"She's a smitten kitten," Lottie says.

Just then, something scampers across the table and a ball of fur streaks by.

Minnie doesn't squeak this time. She screams.

Hazel, a tall and seemingly capable, confident woman, leaps into my arms and I'm cradling her.

Colette stands on a nearby chair, shouting, "Mouse, mouse."

Tyler gazes wistfully at Minnie.

Hazel huffs. "No, not Minnie. A mouse just ran across the dining room table."

"Go get it, Mew," Lottie hollers, appearing with a broom.

Hazel's eyes lock with mine as if we momentarily forgot about the chaos in the room.

She opens and closes her mouth as if to say something.

"I got this," I say and gently set Hazel down, but not before taking note of how perfect she felt in my arms. Her soft skin, her long legs, the way she gazed at me. Okay, maybe she was terrified, but I felt like a regular Captain America.

I empty a bowl of popcorn dotted with candy hearts, grab one of the stiff placemats, and take control of the situation.

"Please, don't kill it," Minnie says, her voice small.

"Catch and release," I say, waving my makeshift tools in the air.

The cat has the poor creature cornered. I angle the bowl over it and then nudge it with the placemat before making a seal to contain the mouse.

The girls cheer. Hazel looks relieved.

Tyler and I, the heroes of the hour, march outside to the park across the street and let the little mouse go.

We bond as we head back in.

"That really worked up an appetite," Tyler says, mock-flexing his arms. "Thanks for doing the heavy lifting though."

I chuckle because we both know there is nothing heavy about a small rodent.

When we return to the dining room, the girls cleared the table. "Where is the food?"

Colette shakes her head. "Mickey Mouse contaminated our brunch."

"We called for takeaway," Lottie says.

"Thank you for saving the day," Hazel says as she slouches on the couch.

"I have two sisters and they're not overly fond of things that creep, crawl, or scamper. The number of spiders I had to rescue," I say, throwing air quotes, "should gain me nothing short of sainthood if there is such a thing in the spider-world."

"There isn't," Minnie mumbles.

I shrug, glancing around at the forlorn faces.

"Hang on," I rush down the hall to my apartment and return with another plate of cookies. These are a tiny bit browner than I'd like around the edges, but by the sound of cheers in the room, this doubles my hero status.

Hazel gives me a look. I can't tell if she's more grateful for rescuing her house from the mouse or if she's thankful that I had a second cookie supply.

"It really helps to have friends who bake."

"Speaking of..." Lottie starts talking about her favorite baking contest reality show.

They all chat while Tyler and I bond over how manly we are. Actually, not really. We discuss our fantasy football teams. The guys at work coaxed me into participating, not realizing I have an uncanny knack for picking winners whether it comes to investments or athletes...or women.

Rather, a woman. Because the gal across the room has somehow captured my candy heart...and apparently kept my contact page open on her cell phone. Does that mean she was going to invite me over for this Galentine's Day soiree or for some other reason?

After I joined the clean plate club, learned that Lottie also loves to bake, Hazel loves to eat and that Mew, Hazel's cat, loves me, I reluctantly leave. Hazel shoos us all out of her apartment because she has to get ready to teach a yoga class early this evening.

I clean up my baking mess and then log onto my laptop to review a few things for work. I slide over to my fantasy football team and get an advertisement for a baking club. Then another for a pastry cookbook and a third for the baking television show Lottie was talking about. I click on it and go down a rabbit hole of deliciousness.

I'm not ready to turn in my certified *stud* card for one that says something along the lines of *baking nerd*. I figure I'll stop soon. The thing is, I'm hooked. They say caffeine, nicotine, and sugar can be addictive. They don't mention measuring, mixing, and kneading as equally so...or the girl next door.

It's creepy how the internet knows what I've been up to. Probably because I was looking up what brown sugar versus white sugar does to a cookie. Need answers? The internet has them plus some you probably don't want.

After I see an ad for a program that promises to transform dreams into reality three times, I finally click on it to see if there's a complaint form or something I can submit to make it go away.

The banner says UDream, UDesire, UDo @ UUniversity.

The tagline underneath says **A program for people who want to awaken their inner spark, discover their dreams, harness their desires, and go after them—and have fun while doing it.**

I chuckle at the internet's empty promises. Nonetheless, I keep reading.

Feeling stuck?

Now that you mention it. Maybe?

I scroll down.

Uninspired?

Sometimes.

I continue to scroll.

Confused?

Hazel's image pops into my mind and my chest lurches. *Uh, huh.*

Know there is potential in you and talents untapped, but not sure how to access them?

This website isn't speaking my language, but I can't bring myself to click away. It has a certain charm, charisma, confidence. It's the kind of stuff I learned on the job. What if I'd had this when I was just out of college, made more mistakes than I'd like to admit, and routinely made a fool of myself by trying to prove something to the higher-ups at the office.

I found my innate confidence, but curiosity about how others might find it too leads me to continue to read. My grandfather used to say, "A rising tide lifts all ships."

When I get to the bottom of the page, I read that same quote in big blue letters.

Coincidence?

Several paragraphs describe the program led by someone named Professor Loves-Her-Life, emphasizing the importance and power of tapping into the truest, rawest, deepest inner desires to manifest a life from which the student doesn't seek escape.

This might be the kind of thing to introduce to the members of the junior finance team, my assistant, heck, even my sisters. But I could never suggest something without trying it first.

I read several testimonials and reviews from graduates of the program and it all seems encouraging and legit.

One woman left her dead-end job and now earns six-figures selling a product she'd whipped up to reduce ingrown hair. She says helping people brings her joy and satisfaction.

Using the method, a tech guy from Silicon Valley revamped his life, shed unwanted weight, left a lousy relationship, did volunteer work in South America, and renewed his passion for his job.

A third was unemployed and now operates a non-profit with an amazing team of big-hearted folks.

I chuckle. Rarely do I hear the words *job* and *joy* in the same sentence. That's just it. So many of us, often myself included, think of work as soul-sucking instead of life-giving. This program seems to help people reframe their perspective.

My curiosity grows. This could help the junior team I'm mentoring. I press the tab that says *Ready*? There's just one paragraph in the center of the screen.

Being stuck, uninspired, and confused isn't your destiny. Chances are you've tried to think your way out of your situation, but can't figure it out. The solution is to get out there and live more. If you're anything like me, that's easier said than done, but if you trust me and more importantly, yourself, you can do anything. I am your guide for four weeks, reintroducing you to yourself, to the sources of your happiness, pointing you toward joy, helping you reveal your deepest desires, and giving you the tools to take action. I invite you to take this journey with me. The worst that can happen is you'll make a huge transformation and be well on your way to living the life of your dreams.

Mostly, the desire and confused parts resonate with me. But this is purely for research purposes for the junior team. That's what I tell myself, anyway. My finger hovers over the *buy now* button.

I'm not going to lie, my heart desires the girl next door, which is confusing because I'm single by choice. If for some reason I wanted more, I don't think I'd have the guts to do anything about it.

Click.

CHAPTER 4
FLIRTING WITH DANGER
HAZEL

I still occasionally wake up to the screech of metal, heat rushing at me, tears already in my eyes even though I didn't really know what was happening at the time.

I'll be walking down the bustling streets of Manhattan, hear a cab crunch against another car and my stomach dips and flops and that feeling of free fall makes me dizzy.

At random moments, like when I'm having a coffee with a friend or upside down in a yoga pose, *blam,* my world turns upside down too.

Even now, the tears are the same: metallic, hot, and constant.

When I was nine, I was in a terrible car accident. My father didn't make it. My mother was in a coma for three days. I was told I'd never walk again. I was determined to learn how to walk again because my big plans in life required mobility—at the time they involved being a prima ballerina and then someday scaling Mount Fuji, Whitney, and Kilimanjaro. They sounded so exotic and impossible; of course, I had to reach the peaks.

Most people know that I routinely do the daring, impossible, the *what is she thinking* kinds of things but not why. They don't know the details before the accident—my parents had been arguing while on our way back from a holiday party. I was in the backseat, trying not to listen, but how could I not?

My father cheated on my mom, regularly. This was a *secret*—something we never talked about. But she and I both knew. The gist of their fight was while at the party, my father flirted with one of his former flings. Understandably, my mom wasn't okay with that. They hurled words like *unfaithful* and *temptation* between them.

The icy rain pelted the windshield. *I didn't intend to upset you. It didn't mean anything.* The tires slipped. My father demanded to know why it mattered. It was in the past. My mother was crying by then. The arguing escalated.

Then the car slid. The streetlights glinted through the glass. My parents went silent. I remained quiet. The car spun and then we were weightless before I screamed.

Crash.

That was the last thing I remembered aside from my mother saying, "*Please don't do it again.*"

He didn't answer. Was there an apology on his lips in those final moments? Doubtful. I hated him for dying because I'll never know, but the most brutal thing is, I turned out just like him.

Well, I'm not married and I don't cheat. Never. Ever.

However, I DO NOT commit. *Ixnay* on the *ommittment-cay.* One date and I'm done, baby.

Dinner? *Check.*

Movie? *Check.*

Call me tomorrow? *Nuh-uh.*

My mother always called me her baby gazelle—not to be confused with Gisele of supermodel fame—though later, we did share the same talent agent for a time. I run from guy to guy to guy, but never more generous with my time or attention.

When I started regaining strength after the body cast and showed promise of regaining mobility, my physical therapist told me, "Walking is falling but catching yourself with every step."

If love is anything like walking, well, I'm falling and, um, I'm not catching myself. Not catching myself at all. You see, I have to learn how to love again because I'm also just like my mother, a romantic at heart, but *shh* don't tell anyone.

Fortunately, my heart was never broken, not like my best friend Catherine. I've been with some lousy guys, but never got close enough to feel the sting of a tough break up. There isn't another tragedy that marked my teens or early twenties with tubs of ice cream and empty tissue boxes. (Well, a few, but none of them involving my heart.) Although, in my teens, a certain well-known cosmetics company discontinued their *bacne* (that's back acne for those unfamiliar) treatment spray—the struggle is real, okay!

No, I've always kept love out of the game. That, right there, is my problem. Guys, dating, and all it entails have become a game —Catherine's Valentine's Day Date Double Dare for example.

But for me, it's more like *how not to fall in love*. I'm naturally competitive. I'm a born winner. However, suddenly, I feel like I might be losing and honestly, only part of me minds. But that other part, she's tough as nails and she'll fight me to the death to win. So really, I'm playing against myself.

That's confusing. I should take some of my own advice. Goodness knows I give enough of it out.

I wage an inner battle between my heart and the chick that's been running the show for the last decade and a half. Fine, three-quarters, but who's counting?

This is why I avoid love. It gets too complicated, and the truth is, I never want to cry myself to sleep like my mother did on nights when my father was "working late" or away on a business trip. The solution? I keep hearts out of it completely.

Except now. I smell butter. Sugar. Chocolate.

He's baking again.

At it every night.

Teasing me.

Tempting me.

Oh, sweet buttery, sugary, confectionary delight.

I walk to the door leading to the hallway. My hand grips the knob. Mew weaves in and out of my legs and begins a rumbling purr. I take a deep breath.

Step away from the door, Hazel. Step away.

"Want a treat, Mew?" Yes, I talk to my cat. Don't judge because you know you do it too. And what does he sound like when he answers? A cute little Frenchman if you must know. Yes, I do voices for my furbaby.

The leftovers from the Galentine's Day party are slim, but Tyler's box of pastries didn't make it to the dining room to be tainted by the mouse.

I don't need Maxwell's sugar.

Nope.

The smell of freshly baking chocolate chip cookies overpowers the fishy, gamey odor of the little kibbles Mew eats out of my hand. I go to the sink, inhaling the lavender soap and scrub.

If I didn't know better, I'd swear Maxwell is pumping my apartment full of chocolate chip cookie fragrance. No, wait. I'm mistaken. I've caught a whiff of something like caramel. I sniff again. Caramel, cocoa, and something else. Mint?

My stomach does a little swoopy, diving thing and not because I'm hungry—I powered down a burger and fries for dinner after the yoga class, thank you very much. I'd fallen asleep on the couch, reading. What can I say, Catherine has quite the library in her room. Also, we're getting another snowstorm—a record for Manhattan. I can't help but be slightly jealous of Catherine gallivanting around Italy with her real-life Romeo.

But oh! That smell! It's heavenly. Divine. *Help me.*

I lift the pastry box lid and bite the inside of my cheek. Hmm. They look a little past their prime.

Fine, maybe just one cookie or whatever it is Maxwell is baking for a late-night snack.

I step into the hall, closing the door behind me. I take another deep breath and steel myself. *I will resist the man candy. I will resist the man candy.* This is my mantra. I'm a yoga teacher who's all about empowerment.

I lift my hand and knock delicately. Maybe he won't hear me. The war within rages.

Heavy footfalls approach.

It's not too late to go back. I can make it to my door in four long strides if I sprint. I've counted.

The door whooshes open.

A red apron hangs loosely around Maxwell's neck. He wears a fitted white T-shirt that highlights what must be an ample amount of time spent at the gym.

Mayday

Mayday.

For the love, please save me.

The smirk slays me on the stoop. Or carpet. Whatever. I grip the doorframe, staring at his knockout biceps, his strong, toned forearms, and hands that look capable of more than rolling out dough.

His eyes flit from my mouth to my eyes. I fear we objectify each other—amounting to little more than the sum of our parts. Two people are attracted to the other's appearance. That's normal. I graduated with a Ph.D. in theology and women's studies. It's considered acceptable if it's mutual. Right?

My hair is in a messy bun, my oversized sweatshirt hangs off one shoulder, and my leggings leave little to the imagination. Also, I kicked off my slippers and have on snow boots. *Way to complete the cute look, Hazel.* Maxwell must think I live in pajamas and yoga clothes. I was once a top model and have a closetful of clothing to prove it.

One of our first conversations, when I blathered on about

getting married someday, rushes at me like a freight train down a church aisle.

No. This level of intensity isn't normal.

"Hey, there." Maxwell's voice is low at this late hour.

Run, Hazel, run while you can!

"Did you come over for a cookie?"

I make a non-committal noise. Catherine would call it the sound of longing. I just want a cookie, I tell you! Or a brownie or whatever it is he's baking.

Maxwell steps out of the doorway to let me in. My hand brushes against his bare arm.

I fan myself. The cranking oven has nothing on my temperature spike. I tell my stupid heart to stop thundering in my chest. I need a distraction.

Then a loud boom sounds from somewhere outside. The lights go out. Like with the mouse, I shriek. Once more, I launch myself into Maxwell's arms.

CHAPTER 5
THE WEATHER OUTSIDE IS FRIGHTFUL
HAZEL

Once more, I'm held aloft in Maxwell's arms. During my dancing days, I was dangerously slender because of the pressures befitting the ideal ballerina size. Now, I'd say I'm fitness model substantial. I can hike, bike, and swim long distances even though my preferred state is, as it turns out, right here. In Maxwell's arms.

I've gone mad. Nuts. Off the rails.

The first time, I blamed the mouse. This time, well, the weather outside is frightful.

"The heavy snow from the storm must've knocked out a transformer or something." I lift and lower a fraction as Maxwell shrugs.

Then our gazes meet. I can't tell the shade of his eyes in the dim light filtering through the window. But his eyes are bright, practically sparkling. My body relaxes in his grip as if I feel safe here.

Do I?

His shoulders are powerful. His neck muscles flex. But it isn't like he's straining at all. Not even breaking a sweat. I could stay here all night.

Maxwell smells like refinement. A man who can take care of

himself...and the woman he loves. It's soap and sweets and the spice of aftershave. I stop short of nuzzling against his chest.

Wake up, Hazel. Your heart is not safe in this man's hands.

I shake myself out of my stupor. What am I thinking? No way can I let myself get comfortable. To be tempted by his tasty treats. I have a copy of Catherine's grandmother's cookie recipe for goodness' sake. I don't need his delicious bakes.

After a forced clearing of my throat, I say, "Um, you're still holding me."

Maxwell blinks a few times. "Oh. Right."

My legs are wobbly when I stand again and my core temperature drops a few degrees without the warmth of his touch.

Simmer down, Hazel.

He flips his phone's flashlight on. His eyes are the lightest shade of brown possible without being another color. But what color? Something all their own. I sigh.

I said simmer down.

I follow the bob of Maxwell's phone as we walk down the hallway. The lingering aroma of cookies baking contrasts to the stainless steel in the kitchen as I take a peek in passing. Maxwell's apartment is the epitome of modern masculinity with moody grays and cold angles.

We reach the large floor to ceiling windows facing the street and the park below. Whereas my apartment captures the shabby chic of old-world Manhattan in all its restored glory—complete with tin ceilings, a clawfoot tub, and subway tile—his is contemporary and edgy. It's like he doesn't want to let himself get too comfortable.

I get it. I do.

Yet, I have the faint thought that I could be comfortable with him...and vice versa.

"What kind of investment banker bakes?" I belatedly realize I've said this out loud.

"The best one in the world, that's who." A snicker escapes Maxwell's lips.

I raise my eyebrows. Cocky too. I admit I like it. You know how they say opposites attract. That's not what's happening here. We are not opposites. More like cut from the same cloth and I don't mind. Not a bit. But how would this work? We certainly don't repel each other.

Whoa, girl. You're getting ahead of yourself. Best rein it in. Pronto.

One by one, the surrounding building lights go out like dominos falling. Me too. While I was still in my apartment, I accidentally knocked the end-piece over and have watched the slow slide of each rectangular piece, one knocking into the next, until I found myself in Maxwell Davis's capable arms.

"My turn," he says, drawing me from my very odd and introspective thoughts.

Hey, it's what I do and the reason behind why I'm so successful that I can afford an apartment like this. Catherine has no idea the cost of the rent. Her "half" is more like a quarter. But for me, it's money well spent because she reconnected with her one true love. Mission accomplished.

"Your turn what?" I ask Maxwell, recalling he'd asked me a question.

Without all the light pollution, the clouds in the night sky come into focus. Behind them are the stars which would be a rare sight in the city if the sky was clear. But right now they seem somehow closer. Right here in this room with us.

Once more our eyes meet and this time he delays in coming up with a reply.

We're standing shoulder to shoulder as if ignoring the fact the power outage brought us in here. Instead, we're speaking in soft voices as if we're trading secrets.

My heart beats rapidly.

"The game you were playing earlier at the Galentine's Day party—wasn't it some version of truth or dare?"

My stomach plunges as I remember whose name I wanted to fill in the blank with in response to the question: *When I think about ______ I get all mushy inside.* Yeah, he's standing right in front of me. And of course, he saw his contact page on my phone. He put it there, but that was days ago. He knows that there's no chance it would still be open unless I'd opened it.

I go still. Is this karma or whatever for basically forcing Catherine to date? Did she hex me? In reality, I don't believe in stuff like that, but I reserve the right to ask questions.

Finally, I manage to speak. "Oh, that. My friends are on an endless quest to embarrass me. It was nothing." I wave my hand dismissively.

"Did it have something to do with that dating dare? What was the deal with that?"

Relief whooshes through me like the snow swirling out the window. I thought he was going to push for me to fill in the blank. That's a no go. Or maybe he's simply sparing us an awkward moment. Yep. That's the one. The guy knows exactly what he's doing. Smooth as silk.

Maxwell leans casually against the wall next to the window. An amused smile plays on his lips as if he's not letting me off the hook. A powerful businessman like him didn't get to a place in his career where he can afford an apartment like this by being unobservant. Nope. He was paying attention and when I least expect it, he'll spring the question about the fill in the blank.

But like I said, we're a lot alike. This isn't a game of dominos. This is a chess game, and I'm the queen.

I'll play all my pieces before I allow him to enter checkmate. Yes, my ego is that huge and that guarded.

"Here's the deal. Catherine had experienced a nearly decade long dry spell. No dates, boyfriends, or kissing since college. Every now and again, I'd try to set her up with someone, but it didn't work out. She'd reduced her dating life to book boyfriends. When we moved in together, something had to change. I had to do something drastic. The girl was unhappy and lonely. Her idea of a fun night was reading."

"You don't like to read?" he asks incredulously.

"Actually, it's in my top five favorite activities, but she

preferred fictional men to real-life relationships. You know, paper princes. Anyway, I dared Catherine to live a little more. A New Year's resolution of sorts. The dare went like this: she had to go out with the first five guys she saw the following morning and pick one to be her Valentine's Day date."

"And I was one of them?"

"Yes, but by then I knew who her one true love was so I couldn't very well have her go on a date with you, but I also couldn't let her realize I knew. She's stubborn."

Maxwell nods as if a clearer understanding of our couples' yoga night dawns.

I will not think about his tight hamstrings (occupational hazard) or his cut arm muscles (another kind of hazard altogether). I will not.

"There was you. Then there was a bum, but I gave her a pass on him—he was leaning heavily on a shopping cart and I didn't want to be responsible if he fell over and crushed her. Catherine is tiny. Plus, hygiene standards and all that."

Maxwell chuckles.

"Anyway, then there was the Man-bun-barista, a total fail. A personal trainer, the Gym Stud where I teach yoga, was next. Omar turned out to be entering seminary so that didn't work out. But because I got a Ph.D. in theology, we've become good friends, so that's an upside. Then there was the Bookstore Boyfriend. He was an absolute lying, stealing toad." I pause. "The lying, stealing part. He's not actually an amphibian. Though I suppose in this city, you can never be too careful."

I'm rambling, but Maxwell leans in slightly as if what I'm saying fascinates him and not because he wants a second date or a kiss at the end of the night. Though I'd be a lying, stealing toad if I said I wouldn't like that.

Hazel, that little voice warns.

"And then there was her OTP," he says.

I snap my fingers. "You've kept up. Yup. The one. The only. The OTP." I go on to tell him how Kellan was Catherine's high school crush and some of what came since, landing them in Italy on Valentine's Day.

"Sounds like an unexpected love story." The softness in his voice when he speaks settles my shoulders, loosens knots in my neck. A breath comes from the depths of my chest.

"A love story," I repeat. "Very much so."

Once more, I lose myself in Maxwell's eyes.

He says, "So Catherine prefers to spend her Saturday nights reading, but you didn't earn a Ph.D. by going out every Saturday night."

He's a master chess player. "True." I suddenly feel I'm on the stage under a spotlight. I forgot my lines. I'm supposed to be the easy-breezy-don't call me tomorrow or next week girl. I'm not a tend and befriend type.

I study the snow as the wind carries it in spirals and irregular shapes as though it's not sure where it's going. Me neither.

My head rests against the window frame. My pulse quickens at the thought that I could snowgaze with Maxwell every night. What is happening to me?

His just barely brown eyes meet mine in the low light.

This is where I'm supposed to flutter my lashes flirtatiously and say something to direct the conversation where I want it to go. But you know what? A quote my mother used to say trickles into my mind. "Don't push the river, it flows by itself." In other words, don't force anything. Go with the flow.

Maxwell looks at me like I'm the only girl in the room. It's relatively dark in here, but I'm pretty sure I am. This is different though. It doesn't feel like he's thinking about someone else or enjoying the view because this is a onetime deal—a take a photo so you'll never forget kind of situation. That flow of time, of ease, seems to stretch and stretch. Forever. 'Til death do us part.

I shiver.

The idea of forever? That's a long time. It terrifies me. What-ifs amounting to everything that can go wrong between now and forever cram my mind.

"Cold?" Maxwell asks.

Before I answer his arm is over my shoulder.

I use every ounce of focus not to shiver again—this time with delight.

Nope. Not cold. Not at all. Hot. Very hot. Hot all over. An inferno. Burning up. "I should go check on my cat." I leave off the part *before you have to call the fire department to douse the flames.*

What is this man doing to me? If Catherine put a hex on me, maybe he's an evil sorcerer. I shake my head because I'm wrapped snuggly under his arm and it's so perfect there's no way his intentions are ill.

The snowflakes dance in the night sky. A few land on the window as though begging to come inside. I press my hand to the glass. "Snow showers at night have always seemed more magical to me. Like the stars are raining down. When I was a little girl, I once got in trouble for opening the window after I was supposed to be asleep, holding out my hand, and catching the snow in my palm. It always felt like a magical moment." I sigh a sleepy sigh.

I glance over at Maxwell. "This feels like a magical moment." His voice is low, rough.

My body is tired but not my mind. It's wired and whirring with thoughts. I didn't expect him to say that.

Amusement plays on his lips. I could kiss him. Then, according to my set of rules, I'm supposed to walk away. Never to be seen again. But we're neighbors and this is...this is something else.

"I should head home," I force out.

"Take a few cookies," he says.

My pulse pounds in my ears as I do everything in my power not to race down the hall.

He passes me a few cookies wrapped in a napkin.

Our fingers brush.

My pulse stops.

His gaze flits to mine.

"Goodnight," I croak and exit.

In four long strides, I reach my door, ready to crawl into bed and throw the covers over my head because I have no idea what's happening, but the knob doesn't budge. I push on it. Nothing. I jiggle the handle.

Panic seizes me. I'm locked out. I slowly turn to see Maxwell leaning in his doorway. I press my lips together and nod. "It was an accident. I swear."

He hooks his finger, summoning me back.

CHAPTER 6
HAZELNUT
MAXWELL

I'm not going to analyze what's going on. Or what I'm doing. Why I'm doing it. Or if I've gone mad. Madmax. Nope. None of that.

Instead, I grab my heaviest parka and pass it to Hazel along with a hat, scarf, and gloves. She seemed especially chilly earlier when she shivered so I don't want her to be uncomfortable. Putting my arm around her was instinct. One that came from some unexplored part of me. I'm a gentleman through and through, but not the kind of guy for gestures like that—ones that force proximity and suggest a deeper kind of care for her welfare. I could've gotten her a sweater or blanket. I gave her my warmth.

I dam up the stream of thought because I told myself not to analyze whatever is going on.

Donning another winter jacket, I lead her into the hall, and to the stairwell to the roof. When we get to the top, I push open the door and we step into the storm.

There's probably an analogy here, something about the storm within, the one taking out the electrical currents I wired to protect my circuitry. Now, I'm forced to go by instinct, candlelight—it illuminates parts of myself previously kept in the dark.

Do. Not. Analyze.

Instead, I look at Hazel, an angel in the snow. She's drop-dead gorgeous with lovely cheekbones, full lips, silky dark hair, and sapphire blue eyes under eyebrows that can slay a man with even the slightest lift. She's sweet and fierce, and I've never met a woman like her.

Realizing my intention for bringing her up here, she holds out her hand as the snow dances down. Somewhere hidden under the blanket of snow is a jacuzzi in the section of the roof that came with my condo. That'll have to be for another time.

Hazel laughs as she twirls slowly. She's so graceful. I could sit with her, talk with her, spend hours, days, months...forever with her?

A plow truck rumbles by below, snapping me back to reality. I have regular business trips that take me all over the country and abroad. There is also the potential for a very unusual event planned in a few weeks. I don't have time for romantic dalliances or long-term commitments. I'm not that kind of guy.

I'm not husband material. That's my brother.

I'm not planning to be a parent. That's my sister.

I'm the fun guy, the uncle, the one to spoil the kids, and travel whenever I want to. To do whatever I want to. But what do I want? The horizon of my life suddenly feels bleak, empty, and lonely without someone to share it with.

My eyes land on Hazel. Mirth fills her smile. She laughs as she flurries over to me and takes me by the hands. Like the swirling snowflakes, we spin in a circle before landing on our backs in the foot of fluff piled on the roof.

Hazel sighs as she gazes up. Even though this is silly and it's cold, I settle, relax. Then she takes my hand and we wave them up and down across the surface of the snow.

"Move your legs too to make snow angels."

She's so fun. So playful. So perfect.

"Yours is a little wonky," she says, pointing at the lopsided wing.

"Hey, be nice," I say, joking. Then I crouch, scoop up a handful of snow, and ball it up.

Her eyes widen in recognition and she does the same.

I lob my snowball toward her arm.

She whirls and tosses, missing me as a smile lights up her face. She takes shelter behind a pile of outdoor furniture.

I duck behind a piece of the building's machinery on the roof and scoop up more of the snow, pat it into a ball, and watch for her to make a move.

With a mock-battle cry, she emerges from behind her hideout and tosses a snowball at me. Misses again. I realize now, that was a distraction. It's too late as I try to remain undercover as she charges forward—a Nordic warrior princess. From her other hand, she lobs a snowball squarely at my chest, nailing her target.

I'm done for. Sunk. A man down.

No, not because of the snow but this woman. She's melted me inside and out.

I follow her laughter as I make chase, picking up snow as I go, hastily shaping balls, and letting them fly. She must've made a stash by the outdoor lounge chairs because she slides behind them and more snow sails through the air.

Once more, she clobbers me with three perfectly aimed snowballs. But I wage a sneak attack and get her in the leg, backside, and arm.

She races to her furniture fort but slips and her arms windmill as she tries to get her footing. Forget this snowball fight, I have to save my woman. It's too late for me to catch her on her feet, but I rush forward, sliding in the snow like a baseball player into home plate. My goal is to cushion her fall.

Hazel lands on me in a soft, slow-motion drop.

"Are you okay?" I ask. I didn't hear any bones cracking or cries of pain.

"I think so." She pats herself and then my chest.

We're tangled up in a warped yoga pose with Hazel on her

side. I'm on my back. Thanks to the snow on the roof and our heavy winter gear, we both have all parts intact.

On second thought, I'm not so sure that's true.

Hazel lets out a long, cold breath that clouds the air. As has happened so many times this evening, our eyes meet. It's like neither one of us can ask the questions, say the words, convey how we feel. Maybe it's because we're not sure. This is uncertain ground.

With an extended hand, I help Hazel to her feet.

"Thank you," she says.

"Don't thank me yet," I say, lobbing another snowball in her direction.

"You just broke my fall as a tactic to fire at close range," she says and scoops up more snow.

We laugh and hoot, tossing snow at each other until our fingers lose feeling despite the gloves.

Hazel shivers. I want to put my arm around her again. Instead, I take her hand and lead her back inside. Warmth rushes through me at her touch. Her grip is firm, telling me she welcomes my hand in hers.

I can navigate the ups and downs of the stock market, high-risk investments, and business mergers better than most, but this is all new territory.

"You have good aim."

"Like Cupid." She strings an invisible bow. Then her face falls slack as though suddenly embarrassed. "You know, like Galentine's Day, er Valentine's. Never mind." Hazel presses her gloved hands over her face. "I'm not usually like this," she mumbles.

I peel her hands away, once more feeling warmth at our connection. "Like what?" I ask.

She peeks up at me. "Like my blood sugar is low or like I need coffee or like I'm tripping over my thoughts, words, and my own two feet."

I smirk. Goodness, she is adorable. "You have nothing to worry about."

She shifts slightly as if she'd like to argue that point, but then she'd reveal her hand, her strategy. And if I'm reading her right, and likely I am because I'm no stranger to poor attempts at a poker face, she's as confused about this as I am. Whatever *this* is.

When we step back into my place, the lights flash to life then go dark again.

"I was about to cheer with joy," Hazel says in a tone that suggests the opposite.

"At least they're working on it. I had a meringue in the oven. I'd better unplug the thing because there's no telling when the power will come back on. Don't want to wake up in the morning to burned egg whites."

"I'm worried about Mew. He's over there all by himself."

"Do you have a hidden key?" I ask. Poetry about keys to hearts flutters into my mind.

"No. I meant to stash one but hadn't gotten around to it."

"Do any of your friends have a spare?"

She shakes her head. "And if they did—" She pats her pockets. "My phone is—" She thumbs over her shoulder. "I'll have to call the building super."

"I have his number." I make the call and leave a message. Likely, he's handling numerous requests about the power outage.

We move to the kitchen where Hazel holds the phone light while I fuss with the power cord. "The kitchen is a mess, but I'll have to clean up later. In the meantime, how about a slice of spiced pecan and apple upside-down pie?" I straighten and walk over to the counter where I had it cooling.

"You went from basic chocolate chip cookies to that?" she asks as she shines the light on the creation.

"Yeah, uh, I guess I got all mad scientist up in here." I chuckle. Or using my newfound hobby as a way to allay my growing feelings for the woman who appeared in my kitchen, lured by the aforementioned hobby. I suppose I did this to myself.

We settle in the living room with the pie and I light a couple candles.

Hazel is quiet for a few long minutes. The light flickers, illuminating the smooth slope of her nose, the brush of her lashes, and the delicate motion of her mouth.

"I'm sorry I couldn't warm it up."

"Hot. Cold. Whatever. This is divine. Better than the crazy-roni I ate last time I was in a power outage."

I get a little hit of serotonin from her compliment. If this were a social media post, love hearts would be going up. Then what else she said catches up with me. "Crazy-what?"

"When I was a kid, and we'd move to a new place, my mom would always make this crazy macaroni and cheese thing on our first night. I called it crazy-roni. It would be whatever we had left over from our fridge like condiments and added to a pot of macaroni and cheese. Hot sauce, my emergency stash of chocolate chips, canned peas, whatever."

"Do you prefer shell or elbow-shaped pasta? This is very important to my nieces and nephews."

"Can I say both?"

I chuckle. "Of course, you'd say both."

"Why's that?"

"Because you're Hazel. Hazelnut."

She cocks her head. "And who's that?"

"I don't know. You tell me."

We spend the next few minutes talking about our favorites. I have definitive likes and dislikes whereas it seems like she prefers *both.*

"Chocolate or vanilla?" I ask.

"Both."

"Beaches or mountains?"

"Both."

"Summer or winter?"

"Both."

We go back and forth, getting more diverse and complicated. She always says *both*. It works. Seems true to her.

"Skiing or snowboarding?" Hazel asks.

I scratch my chin. "Snowboarding. I used to ski, but my brother got me into snowboarding."

"Believe it or not, I've never tried either."

"We'll have to go some time. We'll try both. See which one you like." The event up north in Vermont comes to mind. It's random. A lark. Something outside the norm and my comfort zone. I push it from my mind.

"What if I like both equally?"

"Sounds like you have commitment issues," I say around a laugh.

She drops her fork on the plate as though startled. As though I hit home.

I clear my throat. "Takes one to know one."

Her shoulders drop a fraction. "I've got one. Do you like cookie butter or Nutella better?"

"My sister went on a cookie butter kick once. Made me try it. Shortbread and spice. Nothing to dislike, but this is a no brainer. Nutella."

"I'm practically drooling over here. Both! How can you pick one or the other?"

"Because Nutella is made of hazelnuts. Like you. Hazelnut." I slide closer to her on the couch. "My hazelnut."

She laughs and pushes gently against my chest as if to say, *Get out of here* in a joking way.

And just like that, I've decided that she's *my hazelnut*. Emphasis on *my*.

I don't know if this storm brought in a gust of change or if it started sooner. Maybe it was the chocolate chip cookies. Love at first bite or something. Whatever it was, change is afoot, and I just made a very important decision that's been heavy on my mind. Two actually. This time, like Hazel, I'm going to opt for both. I can have my cake and eat it too. Maybe.

I chuckle. "You'll have to make me some of that crazy-roni sometime."

If tonight is any indication, I have a feeling sometime will come...someday.

But for all my confidence and swagger, it terrifies me.

CHAPTER 7
BREAKING THE RULES
HAZEL

Dark gray sheets. My bedsheets are a leopard print paisley combo. Catherine says they're garish. I like both patterns and couldn't decide on one or the other so I got the set with both. My thoughts have a dreamy quality.

Cookie butter and Nutella.

Hazelnut!

My hazelnut.

I blink a few times.

White curtains. I have peach drapes with lacy edges.

I sit up. No, that's snow out the window.

I'm in Maxwell's spare bedroom.

The evening before flurries back like the snow outside.

I flop back and snuggle under the charcoal gray comforter in the spare bedroom of Maxwell's condo. I catch whispers of the spicy, soapy, minty, cookie smell of him. I burrow a little deeper and inhale deeply before releasing a sigh.

I can spend all day asking myself what strange magic occurred between us last night as we stayed up talking under the guise that we had to wait for the building super to call and let me into my apartment. That we had to wait for the power to turn back on. Really, we just enjoyed chatting.

When have I ever just chatted with a guy for hours?

I can count on one hand. I had a best friend that was a boy when I lived in Los Angeles for a short time. He lived next door. Then there was a set of twins in high school. We bonded over our love of Shakespeare and theater. College brought with it Tyler and my other friends. We made a pact never to date because it would be the ruin of the group.

What am I thinking? This is dangerous.

I listen for the shower. Just the glide of a plow and honking cabs from somewhere below on the city streets. If the super unlocked my door, I can sneak away now before anyone loses an eye, breaks a limb, or otherwise gets hurt. That kid from LA fell out of a tree we were climbing and broke his leg. The concern is real.

I train my ears toward the kitchen. No pots and pans clanging.

I roll over.

Maxwell left a note on the table next to the bed. It says:

Good morning, Hazelnut,

Didn't want to wake you, but I had to go to work. The building super left your key. It's on the counter. I encourage you to have a cookie or a slice of pie for breakfast...or both.

-Max

It's sweet, brief, and non-committal, except that it exists. He signed off with a simple dash and his name. No doodle heart or Xs and Os. Phew.

But there is the hazelnut part. Last night, Maxwell said, "*My hazelnut.*"

I swallow thickly. I've never been anyone's *my* anything.

We both dozed off on the couch with our feet on the ottoman. As hours passed, they'd fallen together, resting comfortably, warmly, touching. Later, I vaguely remember Maxwell carrying me in here, tucking me in, and whispering goodnight.

I want to flee.

I never want to leave this bed again!

The battle within continues.

I've gone against my code of conduct. Firstly, I didn't mean to stay overnight. That's rule number one. But that was more circumstance. I couldn't very well snooze in the hall. Mrs. Hess would report me to the building president.

Number two is never befriend a guy I have feelings for. My mother grew up in London, but my grandmother was from a small village in the English countryside. Every summer, she'd visit. She loved the chickens but didn't understand why they didn't have names. Her Gran explained it was so lads and lasses like her didn't get attached. When they had chicken noodle soup for supper, she understood.

And rule three? Never fall in love.

I glance at the note again. The way he broke my fall on the roof. Warmed my hands. Maxwell is so thoughtful. So nice. But I don't want nice. I want...

Well, I don't know what I want. My requirement before was just devastatingly handsome, good teeth, honest and compassionate, and agreeable to my terms: one date only.

Maxwell meets every condition and then some. Of all the men I've dated, no one compares. His teeth are thousands of dollars in orthodontic perfection and pearly white. He and Mew made fast friends, and he's been nothing but sweet to me.

He's tall, tanned, chiseled.

His apartment is masculine and clean.

He's successful, well-spoken, and confident. Very confident but not too cocky.

He's a little mysterious.

Rules one and two? Fail and fail.

And three? Let's not talk about that.

As the snow continues to fall, I realize my error. We're not dating. We're doing something else. I don't know what to call it.

But I'm not falling in love, promise. Maybe except with Maxwell's baking. That I'll admit to loving.

———

After giving Mew a lot of TLC in apology for my absence, showering, and belatedly realizing the power is back on, a long sigh escapes. It can probably be heard seven blocks down, a few streets over, and in the police station. Lock me up. Throw away the key. Save me from myself!

But there is no saving to be had. Just spending—a lot of time with Maxwell.

The night after the storm, he brought over a Swiss roll filled with mascarpone whipped cream and a layer of Nutella. And a Swiss roll filled with buttercream and a layer of cookie butter. Said he couldn't decide between the two.

I couldn't either, but I am certain of one thing, this banker is a very talented baker.

Bash, the Man-bun-barista and part of the Valentine's Day Date Double Dare, has nothing on Maxwell. My guy is a gifted and skilled kitchen wizard.

My guy.

My hazelnut.

Oh, dear.

Brain, back on track.

Or maybe Maxwell is one of those people who tries new things, excels, and then moves onto the next. That gives me pause. What if he moves on from providing me with delicious sweets? Then a tiny little voice that dwells in my chest whispers *What if he moves on from you?*

Way to get ahead of yourself, Hazel. He isn't my cookie dealer. Or my anything.

Not yet.

Shhh!

The rest of the week is a nightly parade of pastries.

Croissants. Cream horns. Cheese Danish.

Have mercy!

That night he brings over vanilla and chocolate truffles. Some have caramel centers, others nougat, and a few with mixed berry fruit filling.

No, Maxwell is my chocolate truffle dealer. They're divine. I tell him this no less than a dozen times. Twice for each truffle I devour. Then we watch a movie. I don't know which one of us suggested it after we debated period dramas. I must be a hazel*nut* because at one point I thought Ryan Gosling, playing Noah Calhoun, said, "Girl, what are you thinking...?"

Catherine's gone. There's no roommate or parent or anyone waiting for me with their hand on their hip ready to scold me for having a boy over. Yet it feels like something to be kept secret. From who though?

Maxwell's arm casually slings over my shoulder as we watch the dramatic ending. Tears roll along with the credits. I hastily wipe them away. He rubs little soothing circles on my shoulder.

I am not this kind of girl.

No, I'm a hazelnut.

From what I've gleaned, Maxwell isn't a dater or committer. That means he's not emotionally available and not interested in sharing time and resources with the same woman. Not that he's doing that now, but he's not *not* doing it. Everything about Maxwell suggested he was the same as me. Date and done. Snuggling on the couch and nuzzling his foot against mine does not fit the equation.

But it does feel nice.

I sigh contentedly.

Apparently, the sound gave him the confidence or permission to ask, "What are you doing next weekend?"

I abruptly sit up. "Huh?"

Next weekend means future plans. That's a no-fly zone.

"I have a thing up north. Want to go?" he asks.

"Oh, um."

Maxwell lifts his eyebrows in question. Likely because my responses have amounted to guttural sounds. *Huh. Oh, um.*

"I also have a thing."

I'm pretty sure he forces a shrug. "No biggie. I thought it might be nice to get away. Change of scenery. Fresh mountain air."

"That sounds lovely, but truly, I also have a thing up north."

My former best friend, Mew, gives me a look. Yep, cats can scrutinize people with the best of 'em. It's not a lie. But even if I didn't have a thing, what would I say?

"Where is your thing? Maybe we can meet up and tack on a day to go skiing and snowboarding."

I bite my lip. He's really onto me and the *both* thing. I just love life and don't want to wake up one day and realize I've missed it, you know?

"My thing, uh, Birch Mountain Lodge?"

He wears an expression I can't quite read and pulls out his phone.

I scramble, trying to remember. "I think that's what it was called. Birch, beech, pine. Some kind of tree."

His lips quirk. Maxwell is onto me like I was onto those truffles. He knows exactly why I'm being cagey. It starts with the letter C and ends with *ommittment*.

"Is Catherine coming back soon?" he asks as he continues to look for something on his phone.

I'm thankful for the change of subject. "Well, if you keep plying me with baked goods, yes. She's in Italy, but she's jealous of this deliciousness."

"Plying you?" He inclines his head. "That would imply I want something from you." He casually lifts and lowers a shoulder. "Just your seal of approval. Hazelnut's opinion of my baking skills means a lot. I also don't mind seeing you smile with a mouthful of chocolate, cookies, pastries..."

"That's so not attractive." I fight the urge to show him some of my professional headshots. Instead, I twist in my seat so I can see Maxwell. See just what I'm getting into.

His mysterious brown eyes light up when our gazes catch.

The strong jaw.

The lips.

I drag in a deep breath.

He does the same then glances at his phone, angling it in my direction. "Funny thing, my event is at the same location."

I glance at the website on the screen. *The Great New England Bakehouse Preliminary Baking Contest. Featuring esteemed judge and baker extraordinaire, Polly Spoonwell. Birch Mountain Lodge.* Then the date.

"Polly is one of my private yoga clients. Anytime she has an event in the northeast, she hires me for a session or two."

"Cool. Never heard of her though. Anyway, I'm a contestant."

Record scratch. "Wait. What?"

Maxwell gives his head a little shake as if trying to rid himself of a kind of bashful smile I never expected to see him wear. "I was doing research for members of my junior finance team—mentor duties. Looking for ways to boost their confidence. I came across a website to help people pursue their dreams and goals. More of a program really. Anyway, I got it for research purposes. But I have to admit I do like baking, seem to have a knack for it, so I entered on a whim. You could say the program inspired me."

I swallow hard. Oh. No. No way. Never mind. Moving on from the mention of the website. There are loads for self-improvement and dream catching.

"So, what do you say?" Maxwell asks.

"Oh, look. There's one truffle left." I pop it in my mouth.

I could've tried any number of other ploys I've used to get out of second dates. But I can't bring myself to lie to Maxwell. Not that I lie regularly, just sculpt the truth to meet my needs.

But what are my needs?

More chocolate.

Truffles. Cakes. Treats.

But really, above all, I want more Maxwell.

"What am I doing this weekend?" I repeat.

I'm moving to another country. Disappearing forever with my newfound powers of invisibility. Leaving town...? Only one of them is true, but all three spring to my lips. I go with an honest answer. "I have to be there for Polly's sessions. She's one of my top clients." If I canceled because I didn't want to be in the same place as Maxwell, I'd lose her.

"That's a happy coincidence." He snuggles closer.

Maxwell makes something in me go all squishy and wobbly. I forget things like sense and remember things like how I was supposed to meet Lottie for coffee yesterday. *Oops. Bad, Hazel.*

I'm resisting him the best I can, but he's holding me close and I feel like I might crack. Break my rules. Go to Vermont with him.

He winks. "Is Polly nice? Maybe you can put in a good word for me."

She is the opposite of nice. If it weren't for high oven temperatures, she'd freeze everything she cooks. I keep this to myself because I don't want to spoil Maxwell's excitement.

His smile warms the curve that connects my neck to my shoulder. There's a name for it used in yoga, but I can't think of it right now. I can't think period.

"Just kidding. I don't want any special treatment. The baking schedule will keep me busy during the day, but the brief says that I'll be free by four p.m."

"I have the private yoga sessions with her early Saturday and Sunday morning."

Why am I encouraging him?

His arm snugs more tightly around me. I'm loathed to admit it's better than the truffles and you know how I feel about sweets. I melt a little more.

"We could hit the slopes after my events and then have dinner," he suggests.

"What about dessert—?" I cut myself off because it's as if I'm revealing enemy nuclear codes. My kryptonite. The missing dragon scale armor.

"I promise to save you some of whatever I make. I'm still

deciding on what I'll bake." His fingers splay and he presses his against mine, gripping my palm.

Warmth flutters then rushes through me. I lean my head against his chest.

Maxwell abruptly lets go, leaving me chilled, and makes for the door.

He swallows thickly whether because he put himself on the line and feels rejected or this is moving too fast, I'm not sure.

For me? Both. As per usual.

"I, uh, better—" Mew follows Maxwell to the door and stops just short of following him down the hall.

Me too, Mew. Me too.

If I wasn't all melty and goopy and loopy over this guy, I'd explode. I pray he never gets the bright idea to attend one of my yoga classes. My students will lose their respect for me when I stumble over words and say something incomprehensible like, *Move the thing attached to your torso over there by that other thing...*

Which is exactly what happens the next day. After breakfast of leftover pastry, I have a roomful of level three yoga students in a flying crow pose variation. I'm also balancing on my forearms, fingers spread, pressing into the mat, my chin inches from the floor. My hips lift, one knee presses into the back of my arm with my foot locked against the other. The other leg extends long and high off the ground. It sounds complicated because it is—just like the way I'm feeling.

I've been called graceful by famous clothing designers, lithe by top yoga teachers, and agile by the guides that brought me to some of the world's highest peaks, but the face plant that comes next as my cheek smooshes into the mat and my feet bang into the wood floor suggests otherwise.

Twenty-seven pairs of eyes land on me in a mixture of confusion and concern.

"What? A guy asked me if I wanted to go away for the weekend?" I say matter of fact. "I can't say no because we both happen to be going to the same location." I give the briefest explanation.

"It happens to all of us," one of my well-meaning students says, indicating my fall, but which one, I'm not sure. Out of the pose or into... the L word. No. No way.

My palms sweat and I take a long sip of water. "Now for the other side," I instruct after they lower down.

I don't even bother demonstrating the other side because my arms are like limp spaghetti.

What did I get myself into?

CHAPTER 8
DREAM CATCHING
MAXWELL

What did I get myself into? I'm referring to the baking competition, not inviting Hazel to join me in Vermont for the weekend.

Okay, fine. Both.

She hasn't left my mind, but her sapphire eyes, full lips, and expressive brow appear front and center in my head.

I'm in my office with the vista of the East River, the piers, and the ferries going back and forth. Butter, sugar, and Hazel distract me. *Back to work, Maxwell.*

My email dings with a notification, a check-in from UUniversity. The self-paced program contains four modules. The first is *daring* (we have a week of "Daily dares" to complete—enough with the dares already!), the second *uncovering,* the third *dreaming*, and the last *becoming*.

An email arrives each day with reminders, inspiration, and action steps. Today, the note says, **Success comes from acting with intention each day.** I read the overviews so I know what to expect in the next few weeks, not that I'm going to do it, but it'll be useful when I share with my colleagues.

The *daring* module is about moving past comfort zones and understanding that we created boundaries to keep ourselves in a safe, familiar place. It says, **Pushing our edge, while it might be uncomfortable, will ultimately make it so we live bigger, more satisfying lives.** The word *daring* reminds me of Hazel.

Uncovering, is about exposing our perceived limitations and revealing our deepest desires. *Dreaming* encourages getting specific about what we want from our lives. And the fourth, *becoming,* is all about taking action.

I don't have time for immersing myself in the course but get the gist. However, I can credit it with encouraging me to enter that baking contest. It's entirely out of character but so is baking, to begin with as well as sitting on Hazel's couch night after night, talking about our lives, dreams, and desires.

The last line of the email says, **Take your time with this process and go through each module individually, but also look at the big picture about what you want your life to be about. Themes for this include love, freedom, faith, family, relationships.**

Hazel, Hazel, Hazel.

I glance up as Conrad, one of my colleagues, enters my office. He tilts his head and narrows his eyes. "You alright, man?"

In my world and for most guys, this isn't a question commonly asked, hence the "man" cushion at the end.

I blink a few times. "Yeah, fine. Why?" I discretely glance around. Everything in my modern and sleek office appears to be in place. My suit was laundered and pressed. Not a button or a hair out of place.

Conrad wrinkles his nose. "You've been acting funny. Bringing in all those baked goods. Hitting the gym more."

"I told you, my neighbor, Mrs. Hess, is a cookie factory. She's a widow. I don't want to be rude."

"Yeah. Mrs. Hess. My gran belongs to a bridge club at Sunsets Senior Center on East thirtieth. Maybe Mrs. Hess would like to join her." The way he emphasizes her name makes it sound like he doesn't believe there is a Mrs. Hess. She's real, but she's the opposite of sugar and nice.

"You haven't been to Javier's in a couple of weeks."

"Yeah. I've been swamped. Lots of research and development." Not exactly a lie, but less focus on finances and more on the culinary arts.

He lifts his eyebrows. "Yeah. Both of us."

Both. Hazel. I scrub my hand through my hair.

"And you've had a look about you." He sits down with the kind of obstinacy that tells me he won't leave until I make a confession.

I swallow thickly.

Hired at the same time, Conrad and I have been stiff opponents in getting top commissions, but it's driven us each to be better. And we have. But we've also kept animosity out of it because we have a lot in common. Or did until he got engaged over the summer—they met at Javier's.

He steeples his fingers. "I think you've fallen."

"That was one of the guys from the twelfth floor. They have to salt the sidewalk better under the awning. It sure does get icy."

Conrad gives me a sideways look. "Not what I meant."

I let out a long-held breath. Of course, I know what he means.

"So, what's the problem?" Conrad asks, adjusting his cufflink and then glancing at his watch before leveling me with his gaze.

I recognize the power move. The cufflink bit was a display of his success and proof that he's a valuable resource who can get things done. The watch, a reminder that he values his time and I should too if I want to take advantage of his generosity and expertise. Then the gaze says, *Last chance buddy. Invest with me and reach your own level of success. If not, I'm moving on.*

In this instance, I already have invested wisely and have more financial abundance than I'll use in a lifetime. What he's offering is friendship. Someone to talk to. An opportunity to come clean and figure out what's going on.

I tell him I'd asked Hazel to join me in Vermont for the weekend. "Things with Hazel started out easy because that's what I do, easy. No repeats, no relationships, no second dates. I've gleaned she's the same way. We make the perfect pair."

"And you've been seeing her for a few weeks, meaning it left the realm of how you keep things casual."

"We're neighbors."

"Hazel Hess?"

I wave my hands. "No, different neighbor. And much different women." Thank goodness. "A trip with her feels a little like a commitment."

"One that you suggested," Conrad rightly observes. "And that's a problem because?"

"We'll be trapped in the car for hours. Then the same resort and—"

"You do realize that sounds super romantic. Dinner by a crackling fire, no choice but to keep each other warm—"

I interrupt his musings. "Who are you, Conrad Stevens? You know I don't do romantic."

His laugh is practically a squawk. "Love changes you, man. When it's with the right person, it's the best thing on the market. For the record, you so are a romantic. Just look at these doughnuts." He points to a recipe I tested, I mean Mrs. Hess gave me.

"Chocolate sprinkles, strawberries and cheesecake, Nutella, and this one here has candy hearts on the top."

"Hazel hosted a Galentine's Day brunch, and they were leftover."

Conrad wears a Cheshire smile.

"Okay. Fine. I'm the baker." I come clean about the baking. But not the other thing.

He spins around so we're both facing the laptop. "Kylee and Conrad—the future Mr. And Mrs. Stevens. Buttercup and Wesley, Daisy and Gatsby. These are some major power couples. I know exactly what kind of research and development you and I need to do."

I peer over his shoulder as he pulls up an online dating website.

"No. No way."

He's already typing at lightning speed. "What kind of woman are you looking for?"

Tall, silky brown hair, curves for days...

I don't answer, but when his stare makes me feel as though a nuclear attack is imminent, I say, "I'm not looking."

Conrad laughs. "Any particular taste in appearance? I'm going to assume you'd prefer she has good hair. Hmm." He taps his chin. "Vocation? Look," he points, "There are all kinds of filters."

I reach for a doughnut drizzled with chocolate and red velvet crumbs.

"Maxwell, we're doing R&D. I'm not suggesting you meet any of the women that pop up. Maybe if you considered what you'd like in a relationship, you'd realize that maybe the one you want is right in front of you."

"Who said I'm looking?"

"Do you want her to share your interests? Baking for instance?" He waggles his eyebrows. "Favorite TV shows? Recreational activities, hobbies, future plans. Someone who makes you laugh. Independent and hard working."

"Yeah, fine. Whatever." I try to be casual. Uninterested.

As Conrad continues to fill out the dating profile, my thoughts drift to Hazel. My feelings are not casual. I am interested.

"Alright, I'm going to launch this thing. Maxwell Davis' dating app profile is going live in three, two, one." His finger hovers over the enter button.

"No. Don't do it."

Conrad stabs the air. "Ah ha. I knew it."

He was testing me to see if I'd let him post it. If so, things with Hazel weren't serious. If I stopped him, well, then achievement unlocked. He's right. Still, I hedge. "We don't know each other that well."

He chuckles. "Watching you these last weeks is like stepping back in time to when I met Kylee. Think about it this way. When a company releases an IPO and you have the opportunity to buy in low, but don't..."

"Major regret."

"Right. So, if this feels like it could be a good thing don't wait for the stock to open at a higher price."

I completely get his meaning, but what if the stock drops? What if the business fails and I'm out of my investment?

Conrad raps on my desk then points at me. "Remember that love isn't quite the same as trading stocks. You can always make a comeback if you don't get a good return and wipe out your bank account. But most of us, if we're lucky, only get one shot at love." He gets up to leave.

"What makes you think I'm a romantic?"

"Those chocolate chip cookies. I could taste the love in them." He laughs. "It's just a weekend. It's not as if you're getting married and moving in together. You'll have your own rooms to return to. A little buffer."

"But we're neighbors, meaning if things go wrong, I'll have to see her if I want to leave my apartment. How do I get out of this?"

"You don't. You go."

I shake my head. "I need to hit the gym. Get a protein shake."

"You've already been this morning and it's, like, fifteen degrees out. You'll get worse than a brain freeze."

"Something hot and sweet then."

"Sounds an awful lot like Hazel." Conrad winks.

"I was talking about coffee," I say.

"Yeah, yeah. Good talk. Let me know how unforgettable your weekend turns out. I'm going to meet with the Schmidt brothers now." His smile suggests he doesn't love schmoozing but reeling in the big whale investors is well worth the long lunch.

At the end of the day, I bundle up and step into the descending twilight and am careful not to fall on the sidewalk. Or fall in general. The only problem is, with every street I cross,

I'm more convinced I have fallen. This means there's only one solution. Cancel the baking contest. Call off the trip. I go back and forth.

I have to redecorate my apartment.

She'd want to help.

I have an emergency.

She'd want to make sure I'm okay.

I have... I have nothing except a bag full of ingredients for a recipe I have to test. Nutella hot chocolate topped with toasted hazelnuts, marshmallows, chocolate shavings, and bits of thin, homemade waffle. I'll need two spoons.

No, I don't need Hazel. I don't.

But do I want her? That's another question entirely.

The hall is quiet when I step off the elevator in my building. It smells like Mrs. Hess's wet dogs and disappointment sinks my shoulders a measure when I don't catch the scent of vanilla and citrus, meaning Hazel recently passed my door on her return home.

I hate that Conrad was right.

While the waffles cook, I check my email. I got another message from UUniversity. This one is a reminder to join the private group where students in the course can chat, ask questions, and support each other.

I'm not sure whether it's research, curiosity, or something else (need?) that drives me, but I click the link. The discussion in the group centers on what the students wanted to be when they grew up. I skim, reading that TrinaT wanted to be an actress. Another woman wanted to be a teacher. MarisaQ wrote that she wanted to be a famous pianist and is still working on it. No one divulges their true identities and it seems like they're all women. ChelseaDigs comments that she wanted to be like her aunt—an archeologist.

The tone and content of the conversation suggest none of them achieved their goals. I didn't necessarily aspire to be in finance, but what did I want? I think back. My best memories were at my grandmother's house where she was either in the kitchen baking or playing board games with us kids. I also recall our time at the cabin with everyone in the family together, the smells from the oven, snow, and sunshine.

My fingers hover mutely over the computer keys but then my timer dings. I can't help but think about how life has a time limit, dreams as well if we don't take action...and maybe love too.

CHAPTER 9
TWO TRUTHS AND ONE LIE
HAZEL

It's Friday, which means I need to a) fake my own death and flee to foreign shores. But living in anonymity for the rest of my life because I'm supposed to be dead doesn't sound appealing. I'm a social creature and a relatively well-known yoga instructor.

There's plan b), which is to pretend I'm terribly ill and can't go to Vermont. I'd have to cancel with Polly—totally blowing my sense of integrity and possibly career because she's fickle like that. Maxwell would probably also want to check-in and make sure I'm still breathing. I fake a cough. No, not passable.

Or c) put on my big girl pants and go through with it.

I remind myself I'm a grown woman and pack my bag with the hope that perhaps he'll change his mind about the baking and me, and cancel.

That possibility makes me feel suddenly hollow...and hungry.

I leave instructions for how to take care of Mew with Lottie, tote my bag through the hall, and go to work.

Omar waits for a client and with a nod to my bag he says, "You decided to go after all?"

We'd discussed the situation at length after I fell out of the pose in class the other day. He suggested I pray about it.

All signs point toward Maxwell. Yet, I resist.

"He's picking me up here after I teach my lunch class."

"He got off work early, and he has a car?" Omar whistles. "Flexible and successful. Nice catch."

"Don't remind me about the car ride. Wait, do you have a brother who also happens to be a thug? I could hire him to strong-arm Maxwell in the alley. He could tell him that I'm spoken for. It was an arranged marriage, and I forgot—"

"I do have a brother. Soon I'll have many when I join the seminary, but I've also seen Maxwell when he dropped off those biscuits the other day. The dude is bigger and probably stronger than me and my bro, combined."

"He's just as buff as you. You're made of steel."

"Hazel, occupational hazard. I notice these things, okay. Trust me, the guy is pure muscle."

"Yeah, I know." I sigh, shifting my weight between my feet.

"You're nervous."

A masculine figure approaches the glass doors of the entrance.

Omar raises his eyebrows indicating it's game time.

I whip around.

Maxwell wears a dark suit. It fits his broad shoulders perfectly. The middle button is fastened. The tie is as neat as a pin even as the wind ruffles his hair. The pants are tailored for the perfect fit.

"Breathe," Omar reminds me at a whisper.

I bite my lip. The nervousness bubbles over.

The door opens and then seals shut.

"You're early," I slur-mumble as Maxwell leans in and kisses me on the cheek.

The room is suddenly twenty degrees warmer.

Maxwell is a gentleman, or he's marking his territory. He doesn't have to worry about Omar. The guy is on the road to priesthood and sainthood should we be so blessed.

"I wanted to take your class before sitting in the car for hours."

"Smart man," Omar says, approvingly.

We make formal introductions and they exchange pleasantries while I fight the fluttering in my stomach, my chest, my toes!

I lead the students through yoga poses, making a last-minute change from invigorating heart openers to mindful stillness, with long stretches and meditative silence. It's the best I can do to keep the shake out of my voice and the quiver in my fingers from being too obvious with Maxwell on the mat a few feet away.

Halfway through, I have a student demonstrate a pose and then go around the class, adjusting alignment. When I reach Maxwell, pressed into downward dog, I see how tight his hamstrings are. Sweat pools on the mat beneath his head. His hands slip. I run my hand along his spine, indicating he lengthen more. I draw his hips back and encourage a slight bend in the knees.

I take a breath. Maybe he's just as nervous as me.

Afterward, we grab coffees near the studio before heading out of town.

While waiting for our orders, I say, "I've always thought you can tell a lot about a person by how they take their coffee. Espresso versus cappuccino for instance. Drinkers of the former are ready to get things done, are on the go, and tend to blend one word into the next in an attempt to say ALL THE THINGS." Case in point as I take my latte from the barista.

Maxwell smiles. "And what about cappuccino drinkers?" he asks.

"They're more inclined to sip their frothy morning beverage over a long philosophical conversation that highlights how smart they think they are."

He chuckles. "What about people who take their coffee black

with a sprinkle of sugar?" Maxwell takes his cup, filled with the same.

"They're the bittersweet type. They tend to see the big picture. People who take their coffee black incline toward being moody and broody. And those who take their morning cuppa light and sweet often use a straw so they don't mess up their lipstick. In other words, they're perfectionists."

Maxwell chuckles. "And what about people who never order the same thing twice?"

"I'd say they're playing it safe."

Something I ordinarily do but recently seem to have lost all sense of reason.

"Any other theories?" he asks as he opens the door of his slick BMW for me.

"Catherine likens men to dogs. Before you get defensive, if you heard her explanation it makes a certain kind of sense."

"What do you think?"

I don't know. "I used to theorize that there are a few kinds of people in the world: swans, peacocks, and pigeons."

Maxwell chuckles. "Those are birds, not people."

"Let me explain. Swans are all about forever. Someday I'll get married, but it's mostly for the experience and the dress." The instant this is out of my mouth, my stomach squirms with the falsehood. "I'm a peacock so you'd better believe I'll be parading around in my finery on my wedding day. But I also like to fly solo—I need my independence, like Mew. However, swans mate for life."

"You're not a love for life kind of gal?"

This time I tell the truth. "I don't know. Then there are pigeons. They're the ones filled with uncertainty. Not really knowing where they fit or what they want only it's not what they have."

"Are you really likening relationships to the avian kingdom?"

"I am," I say as a pigeon pecks at something questionable by a sewer drain when we stop at a light.

Maxwell shakes his head. "There's so much wrong with your theory. First, you can't be a peacock because they're male. You'd be a peahen which just sounds weird. Second, you're a cat person. Birds and cats? Seems like a conflict waiting to happen."

Our laughter diffuses the tension. For now.

Later, while Maxwell weaves through traffic, I have my doubts—about his nervousness. He's all kinds of casual confidence with one hand on the wheel and the other on the gearshift. His jacket drapes over the seat in the back and the sleeves of his button-down shirt are rolled up while the heat warms us against the chill as we head north.

On the other hand, I'm painfully aware we're sharing a car, not a cab. In the latter, if I needed to get out, I could tell the driver to pull over, but if I tell Maxwell to stop on the corner and let me out, he'll just think I'm crazy. Plus he knows where I live. I have to walk by his door every day. It's not like I can avoid him.

As the closely stacked buildings and bustling pedestrians thin, giving way to bridges and broader lanes, I notice there isn't a Starbucks on every corner. The familiarity and comfort fades as we cross state lines. I turn my attention to the interior of the car: a centering practice one of my yoga teachers suggested to help calm nerves and remain in the present moment instead of thinking about the future and weddings and commitments and heartbreak.

Steering wheel. Windshield. Dashboard. A mix of guitar-heavy songs plays through the speakers. It smells like new car scent. Then there's Maxwell who looks too delicious for his own good sitting behind the wheel as he tells me about some of his baking creations.

"Have you been to Vermont before?" he asks. "I hear they make the best maple syrup."

"A few times—to this resort and another further north. How about you?"

"Used to come up here every winter with my family. My parents sold the log cabin when they divorced. Actually, I haven't been back since. When I want slopes and snow, usually I go out west."

We delicately avoid discussing family as tiny snowflakes melt on the windshield. Despite the heat in the car, chills work their way across my skin. The grind of metal striking metal sounds in the distant past.

I swallow thickly. "Can we slow down?"

Maxwell lets off the accelerator with a look of concern. "You okay? Carsick? I can pull over."

I should tell him about the accident, but I say something slightly less difficult only because if I think or speak about that fateful night I'm sure to cry. It happens every time. "I've never taken a trip with a guy before." No, it's a tie; they're both tough on the emotions and the ego.

"You mean not this soon?"

This soon as in *the relationship*? "No, I mean never." That's not what I meant about slowing down, or was it?

He chuckles genially. "Well, clearly we should get to know each other better. Um, I'm Maxwell Benedict Davis. I know, I have a pretentious name." He speaks as if we're meeting for the first time.

"Not pretentious at all," I say with a shrug. "I'm Hazel Aphrodite Loves. You can thank my British, Greek, Kenyan, Indian, and Russian relatives. All family names. Well, my second middle name is Arya, but then it just becomes a mouthful and I can't fill in the little boxes on forms." I will not be telling him about my nickname from when I was at a yoga retreat in India, thank you very much.

"They're all beautiful. Mine is boring. What would you name your kids?"

"Um, kids?" My cheeks blister and my stomach flip flops.

"Yeah, hypothetically. I ask only because I notice people with long or unusual names often opt to name their kids something simple and classic."

"Then I take it your parents' names were John and Jane."

He smiles. "Actually John and Ann, but you were close."

"Seriously?"

"Quite. They're all family names like yours. Tell me more about yourself."

"Hazel Loves is my real name. People often wonder. You can ask the boys in the schoolyard. They got a kick out of saying things like, *'Hazel Loves the locker room laundry bin or Hazel Loves Albert'*—not the prince. Ooh and my least favorite *Hazel Loves poo.*"

Maxwell holds in laughter.

"What else can I tell you? I teach yoga, live next to a hot guy, and my best friend and I have a soft spot for cookies. Chocolate chip in particular. Your turn. What's your job like?"

"A hot guy, huh?" He raises an eyebrow. "As you know, I work for an investment firm. Seriously, you don't want to hear about it. Boring. Baking on the other hand..."

"Except for the quarterly trips to tropical islands."

"It's still work, though maybe you'd like to come with me sometime. I'm going to Turks and Caicos in the spring."

One trip at a time, buddy, one trip at a time.

The drone of the tires on the asphalt between songs punctuates the silence that follows our mutual hesitancy to talk more about real-life outside our baking bubble.

"My siblings and I used to play a game on the ride up here when we were kids."

"I'm good at playing games," I say in a more surly voice than I mean to. The fearful fighter in me prevails. The snow forms a thin layer on the road ahead, and I grip my seatbelt.

"It's called two truths and one lie. Since we don't know a ton about each other—I'll go first and then you'll get the picture of how to play. Just guess which thing I say isn't true."

"Easy enough." I refuse to think about the Galentine's game.

"I've watched every episode of Friends. I lived in Japan for a year. That time I baked cookies, and you came over, was the first time I'd ever baked on my own."

"Friends," I guess.

"I've watched every episode twice at least."

"Should I ask why?"

"Sisters."

"How many Davis' are there?"

"Five. Three boys. Two girls. Your turn."

"Oh, that's right. You mentioned your family at the Galentine's Day party. What was a lie?" I ask.

"I've never lived in Japan."

There are reams and scrolls and stacks of facts he doesn't know about me. "I was a fitness model while I was in college. I've watched every Harry Potter film twice." I weigh the last one carefully. I already told him I've never been on a trip with a guy before. I'm about to say that I've never been to Japan either, but I blurt, "I've never been in love."

CHAPTER 10
CABIN FEVER
MAXWELL

Hazel's previous turn in our two truths and one lie game about never being in love was definitely false. There's no way that's possible. I got a work call, so we moved on.

In the next two hours, I do learn that she was a runner in high school and college, has an obsession with clothing, and that she is not fond of monkeys.

"I've been an extra in a movie, spend a week every summer with all my siblings and their families—" I leave out the part that I'm the only one left who's single and don't gripe about how this upsets my parents. In fact, it's better not to mention them. "Binxy, our Labrador retriever, used to eat rocks and leave them around the house."

Hazel tilts her head back and forth in thought about my truths and lie. "You've never been an extra in a movie. You'd be the lead for sure."

That's the second time she's commented on my appearance. Is that all I am to her? A hot, hunky extra in her life. Voices of doubt swirl. I snap my fingers. "Wrong. I was in the background during a shot when I used to work on the Wall Street trading floor."

"So what was the lie?"

"Binxy used to eat coins, not rocks, and leave them around the house. She wasn't the smartest dog, but I was the only one in the family she listened to."

"Except about not eating coins?"

I chuckle.

Hazel tells me about her love of hiking. "I have bucket list mountains—Elbrus among them. But my trip to Antarctica several years ago quickly taught me that I'll never scale all of the Seven Summits. I don't tolerate cold well."

"What about hitting the slopes this weekend?"

"I'm envisioning sitting by the warm fire with a beverage and a book."

"And what about a bake?"

"Have you decided on your recipes?"

"I had to submit them by midnight last night." I hope I made the right choices. I have to prepare three total along with the other twelve contestants—we're called the baker's dozen.

"And what will you be wowing everyone with?"

"Surprise."

"Oh, come on. Tell me."

I make a *my lips are sealed* gesture. But I won't lie. I have thought about kissing her. In front of one of those warm fires that are sure to be at the lodge.

Hazel talks some more about her travels and what got her into yoga. However, there is no further mention of her love life or lack thereof. Her obsession with clothing is nothing compared to how my mind fixates on that, but I don't dare ask her. That would open up a door I'm not ready to enter.

As the highway narrows to two lanes and then one, with trees on one side and sparse settlements on the other, the talk turns easeful. I realize we aren't trapped in the car at all. In fact, it's kind of nice together in this journey north.

But then I realize we'll be at the resort together for three days. Three days! That means a lot of time, minus during the contest.

What do two people do together for that long? It's a good thing one of the benefits of yoga is stress reduction. But if I ask her for a session, that means more time together. Then there is the ride back. What if things don't work out? I shift gears, putting the road, and my thoughts, behind me.

"You okay?" I ask when I notice she's white-knuckling the center console.

Maybe the idea of so much time together away from our usual routines got to her too.

"Yeah. We're just so far from—"

"Civilization?" I say, finishing for her.

"Something like that."

The trees lining the winding road leading to the resort look like upside-down hearts frosted in sugar. When we park, like the gentleman I am, I open the door for Hazel. A porter takes our bags.

When she bounces on her toes as the cold sneaks between the seams of her parka, scarf, and hat, I draw her closer. "I'll warm you up."

If we were an actual couple, she'd lean her head against my shoulder, angle her jaw up a degree or two, and we'd kiss. But we aren't so we don't. But what are we? What do I want us to be? The UUniversity lessons come to mind about identifying what I truly want in life.

Yes, I'm still doing research. It's for the junior team I'm mentoring. Sheesh.

We walk under a massive wooden overhang, with outdoor heaters, and into the lobby.

Hazel, with her graceful movements now that she's no longer an icicle, looks right at home among the polished wood and rustic elegance of the lobby with stained glass and brass embellishments, cushioned seating areas, and loads of flowers.

At the check-in counter, the resort employee greets us warmly. "Let me guess, you're here for our signature romantic weekend getaway. You both have that glow about you. I take it you'll be spending plenty of time in one of the cabin suites with an outdoor hot tub." Her voice has a bubbly quality.

But it pops in the long pause that follows.

"Oh, um, we're not together," Hazel blurts.

My stomach knots.

The clerk tilts her head slightly.

"I meant we have separate rooms." Hazel's cheeks flame red and she wrings her hands. Her gaze darts everywhere but at me.

"I'm here for the baking contest," I explain.

"I'm the support team and—"

The clerk goes on to rave excitedly about the event, Polly Spoonwell, and how she wonders what they do with the leftover desserts.

I wink. "If they let us share, I'll bring you some."

The gal behind the desk smiles and types away on the computer to register our rooms. "Oh, gosh. I am so sorry. It looks like we're overbooked and the only rooms we have left are the cabin suites with the hot tubs. Consider it an upgrade. But don't worry. There are two private rooms and a kitchen if you need to test any of your baking." I get a wink this time.

I give Hazel a questioning glance.

Her shoulder lifts and lowers. "If that's all that's left, I guess we don't have a choice."

We settle on the cabin suite and for the trouble, the clerk suggests we relax by the fire in the lounge and someone will bring us each complimentary warm mulled cider.

Likely, she's delaying so they can clean the room.

Hazel's comment on us not being together stung and forces me to think about what I want. The answer is simple and swift. Her.

Then there is the reality of how I'm afraid of not only sharing a cabin suite with her. I have a horrific black and white image of us playing house: me wearing an apron and cooking and her with her feet up reading the paper. A warped, roles-reversed vision of my mother flitting around, tending to my father's every whim creeps in. The part about recreating what broke up my parents tightens the knots inside.

The lounge off the lobby has leather seating focused around small tables with flickering lanterns. It's all very magical and quaint. The cider comes. A fire blazes in the massive stone hearth nearby. Music that reminds me vaguely of Christmas carols plays from the shadowy corners.

"This is the indoor version of a winter wonderland," Hazel says.

She is a wonderland. I settle into the chair, my head balanced on my fist, my long legs splayed. "So, we made it out of the city."

"I try to make a habit of escaping every now and then, but I'm a city girl through and through. Though I haven't been back to London in over a year."

"Is that where you grew up?"

"Until I was eight for the most part. Bounced all over after that—my parents were trying to make things work, until—" She goes quiet a beat then says, "Where did you grow up?"

"I'm from Boston, well, Newton, if you want me to be specific. Lovely, snooty—" I roll my eyes. "Do you like the city pace?"

"Never a dull moment. What I want to know is when it's not ski season, what do the people do around here? Where do they get their coffee? No Starbucks for miles."

"I don't hate the idea." Driving up here, I felt my energy relaxing. I don't think I could commit to the rural life long term...never mind. Don't want to think about commitment. My lips quirk. "To hold cabin fever at bay, they're likely to keep each other amused, content, entertained..."

"And just how do they accomplish that?" Hazel asks. I read the words on her lips more than I hear them. I want nothing more than to kiss her at this moment.

The fire is hot. She's hotter.

Another couple enters the lounge and sits a few places over.

"We could ask."

"I'd rather hear it from you," she says.

We are in full-flirtation mode.

If she doesn't want to be in a relationship, be together, or have anything to do with commitment, I can revive my former self—the guy who'd go to Javier's. The charming, one-and-done bachelor I was before Hazel. "I could show you." I leave the invitation there as I finish my cider.

When we step outside, we get the full winter wonderland effect. The night sky is clear and stars pierce the boundless black like lace. The lantern-lit paths glow halos onto the drifts of snow. The air is somehow soft when I exhale.

With my hand on Hazel's low back, I guide her to the waiting shuttle, outfitted to look like a toboggan, to take us to our cabin.

The driver gives us a tour of the grounds as we pass various lodges, cabins, ski trails, and event halls, pointing out where the contest will be held. "You can download the app to your phone or call from your room anytime you need transport," he says when he stops in front of our cabin.

He loads our bags in and I leave him with a tip.

Inside, the cabin is decorated in shades of cedar and cinnamon. It smells of winter and wood smoke. The low firelight illuminates Hazel's soft features.

We're both quiet as if we want to put off the conversation we know we need to have—the one we left in front of the reception desk in the lobby. The one we both seem to want to avoid like a broken limb...or heart.

But Hazel's blue eyes almost say more than words. They say she wants there to be more between us but is afraid. That makes two of us. *Both.*

This magnetic push and pull, a confusion in polarity, a freak of science in our attraction to each other caught me off guard. Do I want to go back to my simple dating life? Or do I want to hold her hand...forever?

I toss my jacket on a chair and pluck her hat from her head. I untie her scarf and unbutton her jacket. Then I find a little patch of cold skin by her collar.

If words won't come, there are other things we can do with our mouths. I push her hair to one side and press my lips to her neck.

Hazel shivers much like she did the night the power went out, and I'd put my arm around her.

Then her arms wrap around me, fingers squeeze my shoulders, and our lips meet.

It doesn't matter whether I'm warm or cold. Awake or dreaming. Breathing or not. Her kiss gives me life. Gives me hope. Makes me wonder whether this is the beginning of the end…

Of life as I knew it.

CHAPTER 11
SECONDS PLEASE
HAZEL

I am a kitten in Maxwell's paws. Our lips press together. Pull apart. I've been waiting for this moment since I first laid eyes on him, but fear it means more than it should. I draw away. Like a magnet, my lips return to his.

What is it about Maxwell that keeps me coming back for more?

His eyes are amazing.

His lips.

His everything.

He caresses the curve of my neck. I practically purr.

The scruff on his chiseled jaw is like soft sandpaper as our lips meet again. I pull his head closer to mine—not that there is a closer; we're pressed together.

The heat of the fire burns between us like we've ignited, lit a kind of connection I've never before experienced.

When we part, I want the action of his mouth pressing against mine again. We go back and forth, seesawing like this between answering our immediate desires and possibly fearing what's to come if this continues...or if it stops. Could we combust? Self-destruct?

Will I be able to turn away, kiss him once and forget him?

His full, kissable lips quirk, tremble and return the connection every inch of my being longs for.

Fingers tangle in hair.

Palms explore muscles.

I am lost and confused and happy about it. I forget about my rules, trepidation, and the stupid thing I said while at the reception desk about Maxwell and I not being together. If we're not together then what is this?

"You are amazing," he says.

I pause and pull back for a moment, studying Maxwell Davis. Long, clean lines of muscled arms and powerful legs. The kind of posture that nothing can sway, except maybe me. I never want to see him so ruined as when I said we weren't together. He looked crushed.

So I dive back in. Kiss it away. For him. For me. So we both forget.

The kiss deepens and continues until the crackling fire flickers, demanding more logs.

When we part, Maxwell stokes the embers and tosses on some more kindling.

I lounge on a chair, wondering if this is a dream. If Catherine were here, she'd be waving her hand in front of my face, saying, *Earth to Hazel. Earth to Hazel.* I'm on another planet. Overcome. Maxwell makes me feel a little heady and a lot in my own world. In our world.

No one is perfect, but Maxwell is deliciously close.

But what if one kiss turned into two? One weekend together turned into two, three, more? A lifetime?

Beyond the window, the snow continues to fall, blanketing the world in winter white set aglow by the full moon.

I try to come up with flaws. Objections. The usual protests that keep me at a dating distance.

There's no such thing as prince charming. He's a myth. Catherine would tell me that I have a habit of finding something wrong with all of the guys I've dated. She'd accused me of being scared.

With the picturesque backdrop of the sparkly scene out the window, quilting the mountainous scenery in a snowy hush, I already have cabin fever.

As if sensing that I'm not quite myself, ready to melt into a puddle and jump out of my skin at the same time, Maxwell sits down beside me, warming me through.

And there it is. *The look.*

Maxwell's eyebrow follows the lifted angle of the corner of his lip. His buttery brown eyes burn into mine, sending a flare that practically splits me in two.

It's the *I want to kiss you again* look.

The *I want to kiss you for a long time* look.

He brushes the back of his hand along my arm.

My breath catches with a slow burn of anticipation.

I get a lazy gaze. A quirk of the lips.

The look.

We kiss again.

I've figured out what people do to ditch the cabin fever.

In Maxwell's embrace, I feel full, complete. No fears, worries, or hang-ups.

But when he lets go? That's another story. All my fears, worries, and hang-ups surface.

Loudly.

For most people, one of their deepest desires is to be seen, acknowledged, and for their experience and existence to be recognized. However, so often people hide. We hide behind careers, relationships, stuff, weight, and stories we tell ourselves. We hide because we simultaneously want to be seen but are afraid of being judged.

Afraid of making the wrong decision.

I'll have to follow some of my own professional advice to dig down and figure out why commitment scares me so much.

Never mind. I know. All. Too. Well.

"We should grab something to eat and settle in early. Big day for both of us tomorrow," Maxwell says when we part again.

His kisses could probably sustain me for a long time. Then again, who am I kidding? I'll take his baking too.

He glances through a brochure listing the resort's cuisine options. "Pizza?"

"Not in the mood."

"Chinese?"

I wrinkle my nose. "Had it yesterday."

He leans against the doorframe, going down the list. "Cuban? Thai? Curry?"

"I'm overwhelmed by options."

"It's a good problem to have."

"What do you want to eat?" I ask.

"Crazy-roni?"

My chest buoys that he remembers what my mum and I used to eat whenever we were in a new place. Maxwell and I are definitely in a new place.

I read the menus over his shoulder. "That pulled pork and black bean taco with pineapple and heirloom tomato salsa sounds yummy."

After a short jaunt to the main lodge and a bite to eat, we return to our cozy cabin. Maxwell seems to want to pick up where we left off, but I hold my hand over my mouth. "The tacos were a questionable choice. Onion breath."

With a hand around my waist, he draws close. "I don't mind."

I do. And I need a minute to think about this. See, the problem with perpetually being a "both" kind of person is I overthink things. Get unsure about which option to choose when I can't have things both ways. I can't date Maxwell once *and* be a couple. Life doesn't work like that.

"As you said earlier, we have a full day tomorrow and you need your baker's sleep. It's like beauty sleep, only more delicious."

Maxwell chuckles. "If you say so."

He plants a lingering kiss on the top of my head and we go to our separate rooms.

I'm too wired to sleep. Should I bother trying? I can't decide. I'm not usually the kind to waffle unless we're talking about Maxwell's waffles. He brought me some the other day from a recipe he tested. Oh. My. Yum.

I open a book to settle my mind, but Maxwell's strong jawline, his capable hands reaching for mine, and our many kisses barge into my brain and combine with the love interest in the story.

A smile pushes its way onto my face as I recount those blissful moments. I feel the spark when his lips grazed mine. The buzz of his touch. I'm electric. Practically vibrating. But I need my rest. I'm facing Polly Spoonwell tomorrow. Never mind beauty or baking rest. I need to do everything I can to bank patience and my wits. She's demanding and manipulative.

Mind-Maxwell won't cooperate.

"I need to sleep," I groan.

A shaft of light beams across my bed and Maxwell's tall figure fills the doorway. "You awake?"

"I'm sleeping," I mumble.

"Doesn't sound like it."

"What are you doing up? As you said, we have to get up early."

He scrubs his hand down his face. "Couldn't sleep."

I sit up and gather a blanket around my shoulders. "Me neither."

The night is long and luxurious in front of the fire. Yes, we kiss again, but we also chat softly. Sharing things I've never told a guy before: there's a ticklish spot behind my knee, I love sour cherries, and Christmas. Don't get me started. I go gaga over the holiday.

Tonight is the thrilling kind of occasion I'd want to tell Catherine and anyone else who'd listen, but this time, something is different. The time I spend with Maxwell I want to keep tucked away for myself; only to take it out like a rare and precious gem to examine during private moments. To relive the delight, the warmth, and the giddiness all on my own. I'm afraid to share it with anyone in case it diminishes or disappears altogether.

We snuggle in front of the fire, drifting and dozing, chatting and kissing. I don't know what's happening to me—to us—, but it can't be good. I'm sure it'll keep me awake for a week to come as I analyze every moment, every word, every possible meaning...

Especially when Maxwell kisses me on the temple, then in a half-asleep stupor (it was seriously late), he mumbles, "You're the best thing that's ever happened to me."

I let the words spread over me like a warm and welcome blanket, but I can't repeat them back.

CHAPTER 12
THE BAKE IS ON
MAXWELL

I drop the soap three times while in the shower. Cut me some slack; it's soap. It's slippery.

I put my underwear on backward. It's so early it's still dark out.

My leg jitters so much in the shuttle-toboggan on the way to the bake-off orientation, the driver gives me a side-eye and tells me he's only authorized to go ten miles an hour while on resort grounds.

I get it, guy. I'm just...overtired, overcome, overly excited?

Last night I stayed up way too late talking with Hazel in front of the fire. That woman captivates me. And today, I'm unexpectedly anxious and anticipatory and in it to win it.

On the first of the year, if Conrad had told me this would be the one in which I met the woman of my dreams and found my true calling as a baker, I would've laughed in his face. I would've clapped him on the shoulder and said *Buddy, you have the months mixed up. April Fool's day is on April first.*

Had I not been up almost all night talking with Hazel, I would've been up all night going through each of my bakes like Olympic athletes mentally play out every move of their event.

Well, I did that too. The mental-baking-rehearsal. Supposedly it works.

Hazel left the suite even earlier to give Polly Spoonwell her morning yoga session. The contest judge is notoriously known in baking circles as Bake-Zilla. I've seen clips of her throwing a contestant's brownies in the trash, telling people their creations are inedible, and rumor has it she once made a grown man cry by claiming his grandmother's shortbread recipe that he'd replicated tasted worse than sewer water.

"Here you are. Good luck today. I hear Polly Spoonwell is a man-eater." The shuttle driver opens the door.

"I'll pretend you said, macaron eater." I don't want to spend another minute thinking about how harsh she is.

The UUniversity modules talk about the power of positive thinking for manifesting positive outcomes because the energy we give is the energy we get or something.

Yeah, I need coffee. And maybe a shot of testosterone.

Balloons and signs welcome bakers and guests to *The Great New England Bakehouse Preliminary Baking Contest.*

A woman behind a desk asks for my identification and signs me in. Then I get a sticker badge with my first name. I glance down at my deep blue Tom Ford Pinpoint two-piece suit. Adhering a sticker to a five-thousand-dollar item doesn't seem wise. I affix it to my white button-down. Likely, it'll be warm with ovens cranking and the suit jacket will come off.

My choice of attire seems out of place when I enter a lounge area with the other contestants. T-shirts, jeans, and sweaters feature prominently. One guy with a bushy beard wears socks and Birkenstocks. They're all chatting like they're from the same small town in rural Vermont.

Fish out of water much?

I've been called charming, but that only works in particular settings. For a fleeting instant, I wish Hazel were here by my side with her wide smile, soothing accent, and buoyant personality.

A woman with short blond hair enters holding a tablet and a scepter with a golden cookie on top.

Everyone goes quiet.

"Welcome to *The Great New England Bakehouse Preliminary Baking Contest.* As you know, I'm Jenna Carmichael, cohost with The Great Ginger. He's on vacation so you get *moi*. Along with the other twelve winners from previous prelims, the winner today will go on to the nationally televised show starting in September and running until the holidays when the winner will be crowned the *New England Bakehouse Season 4 Best Baker Champion* by none other than Polly Spoonwell and receive the sweets scepter!" She shakes it in the air.

My slow and uncertain clap is out of time with the cheers in the room.

I quickly assess the situation.

It did not register in my brain that this was a run-up for a nationally televised show. The word *preliminary* should've been a giveaway. Rather, I thought it was a quaint, small-town event. Not knowing anyone local, I'd slip in and out undetected. I scrub my hand down my face.

Glancing around at the twelve other contestants, I get the uneasy feeling they all have a leg up, in that they knew what they were getting into, and have binged the previous three seasons of the show repeatedly. And they have some idea who The Great Ginger is. I'm baking blind.

Jenna rattles on with the kind of energy and enthusiasm that shouldn't be allowed in the predawn hour. She outlines the itinerary for the day, including the assigned style of the item to bake, which I knew because I had to send my baking choices via email. In case anyone forgot, it's projected on a screen behind Jenna.

Saturday (Day 1)

Bake 1: Breakfast pastry, any style but must involve cream and berries.

Lunch break

Bake 2: Cake, Cookies, or Bread, any kind but must include chocolate.

Sunday (Day 2)

Bake 3: *The Crowning Glory*. This is when anything goes, but must have baked elements, be entirely edible, and must wow esteemed judge Polly Spoonwell.

Jenna goes on to explain, "Ms. Spoonwell will judge each round, naming a first, second, and third-place winner. They will get an honorary mention on *The Great New England Bakehouse Preliminary Baking Contest* website." Everyone claps.

I'm taking this seriously, but the other people are seriously devoted. Looking back, I entered because this is out of my comfort zone. Put me in a boardroom with high-powered executives and billionaires wearing stiff suits and I'm golden. This is new territory...and very crunchy. Although the woman with coiffed white hair and pearls looks like she could give everyone a run for their money.

Not only is this new territory so is Hazel. I figured if I could do this, I could navigate my feelings for her and whatever is going on between us. It made sense at the time.

Jenna says, "Typically, whoever gets the highest ranking of the three rounds wins the contest, but the third round gets the most weight. Occasionally, someone wows Ms. Spoonwell, and she awards them overall winner even if they didn't perform as well in the previous two rounds."

The guy with the beard stands nearest me and mumbles about season two being a travesty of the treacle sort.

A girl with glasses who looks like she's still in high school says, "Miss Jenna, when will we meet Ms. Spoonwell?"

"She will make her grand entrance at the start of recording and then once more at the end of the first round and each subsequent one," Jenna answers.

"And will we have the opportunity for her to sign our cookbooks? That's what it said on the application."

"Yes. After the second bake later today, along with the audience, Ms. Spoonwell's cookbooks will be available for purchase and she will have a signing line."

After another round of excited applause, we're directed to form a few groups so we can get mic'd up. I get a glimpse of the set, which looks like a classic New England style kitchen with lots of knickknacks. But that's where it ends. Thirteen stations contain state of the art baking equipment. Alright, I'll admit, a few nights when Hazel wasn't around I've geeked out on baking websites. I have the Viking stove, but this collection is clutch. They must move it from location to location during the prelim contests.

After they test the microphones, we step behind our assigned counters set up in two rows. Each has a quaint, food-related name like Sticky Bun Station, Jammy Scone Station, and Sweet Treat Station. I'm at Salty Snack Station. I did once get the sugar and salt mixed up in a recipe. Hopefully, this doesn't portend a failure.

A few dozen chairs line one side of the room and people filter in. Cameramen and women bustle about. Jenna stands at the front of the room by a display of an old-fashioned kitchen with an ice-box style fridge, a replica woodstove outfitted for cooking, and a handmade farm table.

"As you know, Ms. Spoonwell came from the humblest of beginnings here in New England. At her grandmother's side, she learned how to cook and bake. Now, she's the best baker in the country, an accomplished author of twelve cookbooks, and your favorite baking show judge. You too can achieve baking fame. We're going to begin in a moment. When you hear the timer ding, put on your apron, and get started. You will have two hours to complete your breakfast pastry. When you hear the timer ding the second time, you must stop what you're doing. Yes, even if you aren't done. You know the rest of the rules."

I don't. That'll teach me to read the entire application next time. Before I can have another thought, a timer dings and everyone leaps into action.

Tying my apron takes a moment longer than everyone else because I'm struck dumb. The other contestants seem to know to make a mad dash to the pantry, collect their items, and get started. I watch for a long minute while Jenna begins commentating. This must be what the show is like.

Okay, Maxwell. You grew up with five siblings. You know what survival of the fittest entails. Get. It. Done.

I go into the "zone" and come out the other end with a passable puff pastry blueberry cream cheese breakfast braid with drizzle. Say that three times fast.

The last three hours were an effort in endurance and keeping my baking soda and baking powder straight.

A hush comes over the room and a middle-aged woman walks in holding the scepter with the golden cookie on top. Everyone goes bananas, but my attention drifts to movement from the audience.

Hazel stands at the back since there aren't any chairs left and gives me a little wave.

A mixture of calm and sugared up glee comes over me. Whatever happens, it'll be fine. I hardly pay attention to Polly Spoonwell's imperious speech about the importance of perfection. Then she calls my name.

"In third place, we have Maxwell Davis. Who everyone on social media is calling the Banker Baker." She lifts and lowers her eyebrows then looks me up and down.

I force myself not to squirm uncomfortably under her gaze. In fact, it's hard to look at her head-on. Everything about Polly is someone's idea, or more accurately, an attempt at perfection. To put it mildly, she's had some work done—of the plastic surgery sort.

I step onto a podium and am given a certificate with a shiny third place label on it. The woman with the pearls got first and the guy with the socks and sandals took second.

Whatever happens next doesn't matter because it's lunch break and I get to be with Hazel. I push through the crowd as they descend on the array of baked items arranged as samples. The team of assistants put bite-sized amounts of everyone's baked goods in cupcake wrappers.

She wraps her arms around me when we meet. I've never been so relieved. For a moment, I lose my footing and we almost tumble over.

"How did it go? Sorry, I would've liked to get here earlier, but Polly overslept and I had to wait around until she was put together." Hazel uses air quotes. "In our sessions, I try to emphasize self-acceptance, but each time we meet, she has something else—eyelash extensions, permanent eye makeup, microblading."

I wince. "Sounds painful."

"That would be the seven nose jobs. According to her, it was never quite right." Hazel huffs. "She put me in a bad mood. How do you feel about going to get something salty for lunch?"

"Funny, my station was called Salty Snack." I point over my shoulder.

Polly stands in front of the old-fashioned kitchen, watching us closely. At least I think so. Hazel doesn't seem to notice, but she links her arm through mine, and we exit.

When we settle in the lounge by the fire and order French fries with a "flight" of dipping sauces, Hazel lets out a long sigh.

"Is she that awful?" I ask, picking up on the fact that she doesn't hold Polly in as high esteem as, say, Jenna and the other contestants.

"She really is." Then a sly smile blooms on her face. "Although, there was one thing." She brushes her hand dismissively. "Nah. Never mind. I can't say."

I lean in. "You can tell me."

Hazel bites her lip. "I shouldn't. It's the kind of thing that happens to everyone. Also," she wrinkles her nose adorably, "it's not something I should talk to you about but it's..." Then she erupts in laughter.

CHAPTER 13
POOTY POOTWELL
HAZEL

I ripple with giggles. A server brings our French fries and I do my best to regain composure. "I'm eating these mostly because Polly wouldn't dare. She comes off as being sweet, okay, and sometimes shrewd, but that woman is—" I make a frustrated groan. "Impossible."

"The other contestants seem to adore her."

"That's because they're terrified. Notice, everything is filmed and shared on social media. It's all for the likes and follows and fame. You've already been dubbed the Banker Baker." I bite my lip again. "And someone already started a fan page. They think you're hot. Especially when you took off your suit jacket, rolled up your sleeves, and..." I trail off.

No, I didn't start the fan page, but I may as well have done so.

"And?" Maxwell asks.

I stop short of fanning myself. "You made a concentrating face. Like you really wanted to get it right. In my opinion, you did. The braid was perfect."

"I took third."

"Tough competition and it's known that Pooty plays favorites."

Maxwell's brow wrinkles. "Pooty? I thought her name was Polly."

I practically choke on a French fry. "I didn't say that out loud did I?"

Maxwell gently pats my back and passes me water. He's so perfect. Too bad half the country thinks so too. I saw the posts and comments. Women are already proposing to him and they want him to braid their pastries—whatever that means.

I'm about to change the subject but the laughter returns.

He gives me an *I'm being patient, but I'd really like to know what's so funny* look. Either that or he thinks I'm deranged.

I catch my breath. "Okay, okay. I'll tell you. That way, if your hands start to shake and you feel that unique kind of Polly-pressure when under her scrutiny, you can use this instead of picturing her naked."

Maxwell tucks his head back and frowns.

"Yeah, best not to think about that. Anyway, when I was growing up, my mother used the term *poot* for passing gas."

"Poot," Maxwell repeats. "Sounds dainty."

"Well, Polly is not. I'm just polite." Or not since I'm telling him this story. "She was raving about an amazing culinary experience last night and how she'd been out late with some corporate big wig investors or something. She said it was a gastronomical adventure with some exclusive chef they flew in from Paris." I resist the smile cracking across my lips.

Maxwell dips his fry into the curry dipping sauce.

"She was in downward dog."

The fry drops onto his plate mid-bite.

I nod my head and then stifle laughter. "The earth shook, Maxwell. I'm surprised there wasn't an avalanche up on the mountain. In a stern voice, she said, 'You didn't hear that.' But I did. I can never unhear it. It's echoing in my head. I'm afraid I won't be able to teach her session tomorrow and keep a straight face."

We both burst into snorting laughter.

It's not like I've never passed gas in yoga, but it's a delicate release. Not the powerful gust like a car backfiring. Also, we were in an enclosed space and she didn't even say excuse me.

"I won't call her Pooty Pootwell to her face," Maxwell says.

And this is why I love this guy.

I mean...

I don't know what I mean.

That afternoon, I get a seat and can watch Maxwell's full three-hour bake. He takes second place for his S'mores bark brownies, which are a triple-layered threat of chocolate, graham cookie, marshmallow cream, and caramel drizzle.

I take two samples afterward.

I also take notice of Pooty. I mean Polly. She has her eyes on Maxwell. He's mine, lady. Back off.

Polly has told me of her many trysts. Yes, she calls them trysts or encounters. She considers herself a cougar and her ego is bigger than the mountains that form the backdrop to the baking set.

Just as I'm about to nab Maxwell and go make good on our plans to ski and snowboard, she saunters over.

"Hello, Hazel. I see you've taken an interest in my little project here. How sweet of you." She laughs at her pun.

"It seems like everyone is having a lot of fun." They were this morning, but now that they've met her, they're baking in terror.

"Especially my Maxie, the baking banker." Polly coos. "Tell me, how do you know each other?"

My jaw drops. *My Maxie*? I plaster on a smile. "We're friends." Instantly, I could kick myself. It's better than when I claimed we weren't together, but now I've given her free rein and boy does Polly Spoonwell believe herself a queen.

Maxwell slides to my side and plants his palm flat on my low back as if ready to politely rescue me from Polly.

"Hazel, why didn't you tell me about your handsome and talented friend during our session this morning?"

He blinks once, twice, and then his lips quirk. He's recalling the Pooty Pootwell story.

I swallow back a giggle. "I try to keep things professional."

Polly goes on, "Speaking of that, I felt so relaxed afterward—"

Maxwell snorts and covers it with a cough.

Polly proffers him a genial smile and continues what she was saying, "I felt so relaxed after our session this morning that I thought tomorrow, Hazel, you can offer yoga to our entire staff. We won't get started until ten so there will be plenty of time if you teach the class at eight. I'll have the resort clear out space and provide mats." She stops short of snapping her fingers as if someone will magically appear to meet her demands.

"Okay. Do you want your private session as well?"

She shakes her head. "I can't have anything cut into my beauty sleep, now can I?"

I twist my lips into a sort of smile. "Sure. I'll find out where to go from the front desk."

"And this is for staff only. Not contestants. I'll be having a private meeting with them." She winks at Maxwell.

My Maxie.

"Hazel, just make sure you don't break wind like you did this morning. I wouldn't want you to embarrass yourself." Then she glides off.

I go red. If steam could come out of my ears it would.

Maxwell starts laughing.

I shake my head rapidly and my eyes widen. "No, Maxie. I swear, it wasn't me. I didn't poot."

With his hand still on my low back, he leans in and whispers, "Maxie?"

I gaze at the ceiling, wishing the heavens would open up and carry me away or at least cause a commotion so I could escape this embarrassment.

"Pooty. I mean, Polly, thought it was sweet I came to today's event. I said it seemed like everyone was having fun. She replied, 'Especially *my Maxie,* the baking banker.'" I cover my face with my hands. Then I mumble, "I told her that we're friends."

"Is that what we are, friends?" His voice is low, rumbly.

I don't know what we are. "She was upset I hadn't mentioned you this morning."

We're no longer in the event space, but in a long, quiet hall with windows on one side and sconces with dim lighting on the other.

Maxwell scratches the attractive layer of scruff on his jaw. "Yeah. She seems a bit...much. Maxie?"

"You're not mad at me?"

"Why would I be mad at you?" Maxwell leans close, speaking in a low voice. I can smell mint on his breath and chocolate from his second bake.

"The friends thing."

"Well, we are friends." Then his gaze hooks mine. He bites the inside corner of his lip. "Friends and..."

I clear my throat, thinking of the fill in the blank question during the Galentine's Day party. "Friends and..."

Maxwell plants his hands on either side of the wall behind me, caging me in. The snow on the slopes outside the window contrasts with the warmth pulsing between us.

We're exactly five chocolate kiss candies apart.

"Friends and..." Maxwell repeats softer this time.

"Friends and..."

We seal the rest with a kiss. The world and this morning and all my trepidation fade away the moment our lips press together. Maxwell continues to brace himself against the wall and I cup my hands around his strong jawline.

The moment between us begins to deepen when a nearby door slams and the clicking of high heels on the floor draws us slowly apart. I catch a figure with platinum blond hair whip around the corner in a huff.

Polly.

I have to be careful, especially now that she has her sights set on Maxwell. She already tried to humiliate me. I dealt with a few women like her during my modeling days. It's clear that she sees me as a threat otherwise she wouldn't have made it out like I'd been the one who pooted this morning. Like an idiot, I should've told her that Maxwell and I are together. But are we? Neither one of us could say it.

"Those gears are turning and I know what we both need."

Another kiss like that?

Maxwell takes me by the hand and we step into the evening as the lights around the property turn on, casting everything in soft, glowing halos. We get outfitted with ski gear and hit the slopes, remaining out there until our stomachs growl.

Back in the cabin, the fire blazes and we have dinner delivered. I eat a pasta dish with burrata cheese, fresh basil, and a spicy, creamy, I don't know-what-y sauce that is so divine I may have lost consciousness.

After, Maxwell pulls out a container. "I made us our own S'mores bark brownies, the perfect size for sharing."

He feeds me a bite. Scratch that. The triple layers of chocolate, graham cookie, marshmallow cream, and caramel drizzle causes me to lose consciousness. When I regain it, I tell Maxwell, "Now, that's a bowl scraper. You know, the kind you practically want to lick off the bowl so you don't miss a single taste."

"It's second place material." But Maxwell smiles wide anyway as if proud.

"If that's second place material, I cannot wait to see what you have in store for tomorrow."

His smile grows and a silly, mushy thought that is so not typical of Hazel, the world-traveling model with a Ph.D. comes to mind. He's first place to me, but I can't bring myself to say it out loud. I just hope my smile says enough.

CHAPTER 14
FLEXIBILITY
HAZEL

Ordinarily, before I teach a private class to someone like Polly Spoonwell or in this case, a group of people who answer to her, I primp and prepare, meditate, and do a brief yoga flow to get myself warmed up.

This morning, I sprint across the snowy grounds with my mat slung across my back and knocking into my head as I race to the building. I would have summoned the shuttle, but I couldn't wait and don't dare be late. I figured I'd be faster on foot.

Maxwell and I stayed up late talking again. If I'm tardy, the flimsy excuse that I was getting my beauty rest like Polly used when she was over an hour late for our session won't work.

I have no idea what is in store for me when I find Polly standing by the entrance drumming her fingers on her folded arms. She makes a show of looking at her Rolex. "I don't pay you to be late."

I make an apology.

"I have bigger and better things to bake." With a dark chuckle, she saunters off.

I'm practically the last person into the conference room where everyone else sits on their mats, lined up in colorful stripes waiting for the teacher. That's me. I've never been late.

I take a minute to center myself—Maxwell, his eyes like browned butter in the firelight, bounces into my mind. I inhale. I exhale. I gauge my breathing, okay, heaving since I huffed and puffed to get here.

I lead the class through an opening intention, touching on maintaining energy and ease in our practice.

When I draw a blank and a stiff silence follows, I decide to speak my mind. "I often create a class theme based on a topic I've been thinking a lot about with the hope it will resonate with students. When Polly requested I offer this class, I struggled to come up with something that wasn't all about me. See, the thing is, I've had something on my mind. I can hardly focus on anything else." Without thinking, I blurt, "I've never been in love."

You know when you reach the front of the line for a roller coaster or to get blood drawn or do something else that terrifies you? That. Full-on stomach plunging, skin tingling, wobbly kneed dread possess my entire body.

My ears buzz but not so loudly that I don't hear the sharp inhalations, murmurings of assent, and brief chatter from the back left-hand corner of the room before someone shushes the pair.

What. Did. I. Just. Do? Say?

If anyone asks I'm shaking because it's cold in here.

Okay, Hazel. If you're going to humiliate yourself, go all in.

"I've never been in love until now," I add. "I have to admit I'm scared. I'm here to instruct you, but I imagine some of you are or have dated, been engaged, married, or are trying to reignite the passion in your relationship so you know a thing or two about love."

A short woman with braids and what look like pajama bottoms asks, "What scares you about it?"

My eyes widen. "Everything."

A burly guy with a beard and wearing jeans says, "That's not an answer."

"No, but I get it," a balding, middle-aged guy says. "Tell us how it started."

I bite my lip. "That's not really yoga. Uh, I'm supposed to be teaching you."

The burly guy harrumphs. "I didn't come here to do yoga. I came to build and take down the set. I only own jeans and flannels. Polly, I mean Ms. Spoonwell, had the wild idea to—"

"She meant well. We could all probably use some stress relief," the girl with braids says. "It's just—"

The middle-aged guy pushes his glasses up his nose. "Ms. Spoonwell is a strong personality."

A few people chuckle.

"That's putting it mildly," Burly Guy says. He mumbles something about union work and entitlement.

Glasses adds, "She can be a bit pushy and as you see, we go along with her whims because we've seen her fire people for lesser things. Truth be told, I don't want to do a pose, bend over, and split my trousers. So if it's all the same to everyone, I'd be happy to discuss your love life. Sounds more interesting than mine."

The girl with braids gives him a darting and daring look.

"Okay, but if she appears, contort yourself. We'll call it interpretive yoga. Like modern dance." I say.

Burly guy laughs.

I center myself. "I guess it started about a month ago. For the first time, I felt—" I search my mind for the right word. "Stirrings that led to sparks." I tell them my one-date and done dating style and how something changed when Maxwell baked his way into my heart.

For the next fifty minutes, they ask questions and tell me their own love stories to help give me clarity about what's going on between Maxwell and me. I also drop the bomb about my father's infidelity. I wasn't even the one he cheated on, but my mother's pain was enough to make me want to steer clear of relationships.

A few people lay on their mats and nap. A woman with silver-streaked hair listens intently but remains quiet. Others comment about how awful Polly is. I'm tempted but refrain from telling them the Pooty Pootwell story.

When only five minutes remain of the class, I take my first deep breath of the day. The wall of windows in the back of the room frames two snowy slopes and the mechanics of a giant metal chair lift. I find myself distracted, thinking about Maxwell and how good he looks clad in his winter-weather gear.

Then I see him.

And Polly.

She has her arm linked in his as they leave the "Love Shack" —one of the resort dining options where they serve all-things chocolate.

Remember the stomach plunging, skin tingling, wobbly-kneed dread I felt before? It's nothing to how my body knots now.

Someone says my name and then they follow my gaze to the window where the pair approach the lodge.

"That's him?" Braids asks.

"And Polly," Glasses says.

Burly Guy, aka Chuck, abruptly gets to his feet as if he's ready to Hulk Out and smash through the window—he was cheated on once. Otherwise, he's a teddy bear.

Polly leans into Maxwell's ear. Her proximity causes something to slither in my stomach. Then through the enormous glass window, she makes eye contact with me. It's as if she wanted me to see how close she is to him, how she got her fangs into him. Forget Pooty Pootwell. Polly Spoonwell is a snake.

Then again, I'd told her we're just friends. Shame on me.

Apparently, I've said all of this out loud.

"She often picks a contestant as her pet," says Glasses aka Maurice.

"Let's just say the winners do not always have the best bake," says Braids, aka Brenda.

I rush to the washroom and hide in a stall. My mind is a storm of conflict. I want to run away and I want to run into Maxwell's arms and hear him tell me everything is okay.

What has come over me? Why him? Why now?

Someone knocks on the bathroom stall door. "Hazel," a thin female voice says.

I unlatch the lock and peek out.

It's the older woman from the class with streaks of silver in her hair.

"I'm hiding."

"I know. I also know a thing or two about relationships." She leans against the sink and says, "Frank is my third husband. The first one ran off with some young thing." She waves her hand dismissively. "Meanwhile I was only twenty-seven. Oh, to be in my twenties again." She smiles in reminiscence and her eyes sparkle. "The second one passed almost twenty years ago. I still miss him. Frank and I got together when we were already old and wrinkly." She winks.

"You're radiant. You look only to be in your sixties." It's true. The lines on her face seem to glow.

"And that's too old to put up with people like Polly. She and I go way back. I'm Dorothy. The head baking consultant on the show. Polly thinks she runs things, and I let her most of the time because while I love baking, I don't want to let the likes of her drain it of its joy."

I emerge from the stall and wash my hands. "Nice to meet you. Thanks for following me in here—if you hadn't someone may have filed a missing person's report because I had no plans of coming out."

"Doesn't look like a good place to do yoga."

We move to the lounge part of the bathroom—ritzy places like this have settees and mirrors adjacent to the washroom.

"Back to love. At the heart of it is intimacy—letting someone get close to you emotionally. Frank and I have seen each other through loss, surgery, grandbabies, marriage, divorces—we're best friends. We know each other intimately, inside and out."

"I'm stuck on what you said about letting someone get close to you emotionally."

"From what you said, it sounds like you move from one young man to the next, leaving smoldering fires in your wake. It's easier not to get attached, right?" She shakes her head and sets her fingers on my forearm. "Not in the long run. If you really want to live a fulfilled life and have a meaningful relationship, it's worth taking the risk of letting someone in and allowing them to see all parts of you—your fears, wants, desires. All of it."

Wringing my hands, part of me wants to get away from her well-meaning, lavender-scented wisdom as fast as possible. The other part wants a hug and to be told it's all going to work out.

"Oh, and about Polly cozying up to Maxwell? If he's half the man you deserve and have made him out to be, he'll see her for what she is. If not, well, at least you loved and can now better gauge future relationships."

The knots tighten.

As if reading my mind, Dorothy gives me a hug and whispers, "I have a feeling things will work out."

We leave the bathroom and I say, "Thank you for being my fairy lessons-in-love godmother."

I go back to the cabin, shower, and change before heading back to the lodge to watch Maxwell's final baking event.

He's so focused on the Crowning Glory he's creating out of butter, flour, and a lot of chocolate, he doesn't look up. Not at me. Not at Polly.

But she notices me. Polly's gaze slides up and down and she wears a simpering grin as she moves closer to Maxwell's baking station.

The knots inside dissolve. Now, I'm just salty, which is another way of saying ticked off. At her. At him. At this entire stupid situation I got myself into.

CHAPTER 15
THWARTED
MAXWELL

I'm elbow deep in whipped cream when Jenna Carmichael, the host of *The Great New England Bakehouse Baking Contest*, updates social media viewers about progress on bake number three, *The Crowning Glory*. This is when any recipe goes and creativity is encouraged, but the outcome has to have baked elements and must wow the judge.

I understand that the reason they're recording portions of this is that footage of the winner will be used in portions of the actual show when it airs to track the baker's progress. And using social media is a way to keep a captive audience between the seasons of the show.

Clever. Slightly sneaky. But nothing to Polly's tactics.

Jenna leans in and the camera pans over my messy baking counter. "Your fans want to know, how is the Banker Baker holding up? Your hashtag is trending you know." She has a wink in her voice, but I don't look up long enough to confirm it.

"I survived this morning, this should be a piece of cake." It certainly couldn't get worse.

Jenna laughs at my pun and says something quippy in reply.

This bake requires every ounce of my focus. Not because I want to win, but I want to get it right for Hazel. Because I have a question for her in the form of butter, sugar, and chocolate. And because I know she saw Polly and me emerging from the Love Shack this morning.

Because of the early call time to get prepped for the contest, I didn't have a chance to find Hazel and explain. To tell her about Polly's indecent proposal. The truth is, I detest the baking show judge, but don't want to miss the opportunity to say what neither Hazel nor I could when we checked in at the reception desk or to Polly earlier or to each other.

If the triple-tiered cake is any sign, I'm serious. As I measure and mix, pour and pipe, spread and smooth, my thoughts are on one woman. The one with the bright blue eyes, the one with the silky hair, the one whose smile is more delicious than anything that comes from an oven.

I'm doing this for her. For us.

When the timer dings, indicating time is up for bake number three, I take off my apron and prepare to present my crowning glory.

The other bakers have amazing creations, including a layered cake with a rainbow heart baked inside. Another contestant baked forty-eight eclairs stacked to look like Stonehenge, and someone else reproduced their grandmother's quilt out of cupcakes.

When it's my turn, Polly smirks at me then whispers. "It's all yours, Maxwell."

But the golden scepter with the cookie on top isn't what I want. I came here to have fun, to try something new, and to prove to myself that I could, which would give me the courage to move forward with Hazel.

I scan the audience for her and land on those blue eyes I can see even when mine are closed.

"I present my crowning glory because only one woman is my queen."

Beside me, Polly's leg subtly jerks in the direction of the display table and my triple-layer chocolate cake with a chessboard chocolate collar as the base, a red velvet chiffon center covered in whipped buttercream, and topped with a crown made of caramel and filled with truffles topples to the floor. Along with it goes the engagement ring I'd planted in the center of one of the truffles.

Yes. I was going to propose to Hazel.

Yes. It's bold but so are my feelings for her.

Yes. The French-set Halo Diamond Band Engagement Ring is lost in a mass of chocolate.

Where did I get the ring? That's another story, but I've had it since college.

I fight between diving after it and announcing to the audience and staff that Polly tried to proposition me when we were at the Love Shack, promising I'd win if I ditched the yoga teacher and spent more time with her.

No doubt, she realized what I was about to do and sabotaged me. Probably used to getting what she wants. Not this time. Hopefully, it was caught on camera. Although, I imagine she'll realize that and have it deleted from the record.

Adrenaline spikes through me. I crouch down, searching for the ring. This isn't how I wanted it to go. A little voice races through my mind. *Maybe it's for the best. Perhaps you weren't supposed to go through with it. Too soon. Too fast.*

My shoulders drop.

Polly makes a big fuss of the disaster as staff members swoop in to help. A woman with braids tries to rescue my cakes, but it's too late, they're ruined. I spot something shiny, swipe it, and tuck it in my pocket. Her eyes widen in recognition. I give a slight shake of my head. *Please don't say anything.*

I can't recover from this situation now. I'll regroup. Figure out something else.

Dorothy, an older woman with silver hair, plants a motherly hand on my forearm. "Don't worry, Maxwell. The cakes can still be sampled and we have footage of your baking so we can assess your skill using that material."

Everyone is very nice and well-meaning, but I feel dreadful. Crushed.

"I will not be sampling that." Polly frowns and points at my dilapidated cake, a saggy, soggy mess. "He probably did that on purpose to gain favor with the audience." She harrumphs and storms over to the cameraman.

A growl rises in my throat. This woman is insufferable.

Hazel stands on the sidelines and sharply eyes Polly. I break from the chaos and stride over.

"Are you okay?" she asks. "I'm so sorry about your cake. I saw it for an instant and it was impressive. I also saw what Polly did."

I shift from foot to foot not sure if she means the stunt this morning at the Love Shack as Bake-Zilla cozied up to me, which Polly promptly showcased to her social media following or the stunt she pulled with the cake. Either way, a certain circular, bejeweled item burns in my pocket like a beacon.

I say, "This morning, Polly was out of line. She arranged for me to go to the Love Shack. Her assistant told me it was to obtain footage for the show. I knew they had baked goods so no big deal. Turned out Polly was there."

I measure Hazel's response. Green light, go. Yellow, proceed with caution, Red, hightail it out of here. It's over.

Her eyes are sharp and flit around the room. "Yeah."

Yellow it is.

I lean in and tell her what Polly suggested.

Hazel is quiet for a long moment and then arches the severest of eyebrows. "She said that? That was why she arranged to keep me busy."

Fists form.

Hazel hones in on Polly.

Fur is going to fly.

"Polly Spoonwell is a—"

"What was that, Hazel?" the contest judge asks. "I came over here to apologize to poor Maxwell. I guess you can call that dumb luck. Don't worry. I have fired the set carpenter."

"Chuck?" Hazel asks.

"Yes, and the design assistant. While I'm at it, Dorothy, you've been here long enough."

The woman with silver hair fumes. "Are you sure you know what you're doing, Polly?"

The judge and staff begin to squabble. While the rest of the contestants watch in rapt horror, I flash them an apologetic smile before pulling Hazel from the fray to a quiet corner.

I want nothing more than to envelop her in a hug. She keeps a slight distance.

"I am so sorry. I should've realized something was off when it was just Polly this morning. She tried to woo me with baking stardom."

"Is that what you want?" Hazel's voice is smaller than usual.

"No. I want you. Remember I mentioned that online program?"

Hazel toes the floor with her foot and barely nods.

"I'm not the kind of guy who usually does things like that. I'm also not the kind of guy who dates." I gently pinch her chin and tilt her head to face me. "And you're not the kind of girl that dates."

"Or commits or gets led on or deceived."

The ring practically pulses in my pocket. "Which means we're perfect for each other."

"Are we?" Her eyes flicker and land on mine.

"We go together like chocolate and caramel. Apple pie and ice cream. Berries and whipped cream."

"Cookies and milk." The corners of Hazel's lips lift.

An idea for a redo of the magical moment I'd hoped for comes to mind.

"I'll admit, I assumed the worst about you two." Hazel lifts and lowers a shoulder.

I grip them both. "I think the point was to make you question things, to feel jealous. I promise you have nothing to worry about."

"In that case, I should ask, are we more than friends? Are we together?"

"I'd like to be? You?"

She nods.

"Hazel, will you be my girlfriend?" Even though this is a training wheels question in preparation for the big one, the words come easier than I expect.

"I want to be."

"In that case—" I lean in to kiss her.

Just then, a surprised shout comes from nearby. The young woman with braids, face slack, stares at Polly.

In fact, everyone does.

I try to bring myself back to the conversation with Hazel, but our attention remains on the girl who's now crying. I glance around for an explanation. Her shoulders shake as she sobs into her hands. A balding guy with glasses pats her on the shoulder.

"Brenda, are you okay? What happened?" Hazel hurries over.

She wipes her eyes. "It's nothing."

"That wasn't nothing," Dorothy says.

From the corner of my eye, I watch as Polly crosses her arms in front of her chest.

"Was it caught on camera?" someone asks.

"No, but her treachery with the Banker Baker's cake was," someone else whispers. "So is this." I notice they have their phone out. I am not for public humiliation but am confident the very existence of this content might get Polly to back off.

Hazel rubs circles on Brenda's back, trying to soothe her and help her breathe.

Around fitful sobs, the young woman says, "Polly said I was the reason extra-large was invented and that I should lay off the cake and mind my own business. It's just that I saw what she did to Maxwell's table. It isn't the first time either. I can't just keep quiet anymore."

Dorothy says, "No, you can't. It's time someone spoke up. I'm only sorry I hadn't either. I held out hope that Polly might come around. Sorry to say all that sugar went to her head."

"At least it hasn't gone to my hips," Polly snaps.

Everyone in the room gasps.

"She told me we'll special-order a shirt that says *wide load, coming through*. She said I was fat and if I knew what was good for me I'd keep my big, fat mouth shut." Brenda is in tears again.

Hazel and I lock eyes.

She shakes her head. "Brenda, don't listen to Polly. If you feel shamed because of your size, remember this, you aren't fat. You may have fat just like you have a pinky toe, but you aren't a pinky. We don't go around saying, 'Oh, look at that pinky person. Let's criticize her because she's different.' Own who you are and what you look like. Honor that body of yours as a force of nature whatever size it is." Just then, Hazel ducks down.

I fear Polly is about to throw a punch and Hazel is avoiding it with cat-like reflexes, but my girlfriend pops back up with the remains of my chocolate cake on the platter.

"Polly, in case you forgot what sugar tastes like. Try to add some to your words." In one swift motion, she mashes the chocolate in Pooty Pootwell's face.

A long silence follows.

Then someone starts to clap slowly. Another pair of hands join and another.

I expect Polly to go rabid, but her tongue flicks out of her mouth and her shoulders lower a measure. "That. Is. Delicious. And you're right. I needed that."

Everyone, including Polly bursts into laughter.

At that, Hazel and I rush outside and onto the lantern-lit path. The snow sparkles. We catch our breath and laugh.

"That was awesome."

"She needed a little sweetness in her life."

As we sit down on a bench, Hazel's fingers brush mine. The iron in my blood magnetizes to hers.

"I'm disappointed that I didn't get to taste what you baked."

"Me too. But I imagine it tasted like justice."

Her giggle is like tinkling bells in the cool night.

"I didn't realize justice could be delicious...and chocolate. Talk about awesome, it was incredible."

I go on to tell her about my crowning glory, but leave out the part about why I made it.

Her eyes are dreamy in the dim light and we meet for a kiss.

CHAPTER 16
BEHIND THE WHEEL
HAZEL

Maxwell smells like cold snow and the fabric of his jacket chills the burn in my cheeks from doing a brash, bold, and hazelnutty thing. I don't know what came over me, tossing a hunk of cake at Polly, but she had it coming.

Only, there's no time to think about it because once more, I'm lost in Maxwell's lips as we kiss.

We kiss until his lips are warm and mine are cold. We kiss until I forget about fears and trepidation. The refuge of Maxwell's lips provides a great distraction from the bubbles in my stomach.

He asked me to be his girlfriend. I said yes.

An obnoxious voice inside me whines. It snarls. It gnashes its teeth. *Watch out, I'm pretty handy with a hunk of cake,* I warn.

I blink my eyes open, taking a peek at Maxwell. The dim lantern light softens his masculine edges, bathing him in a gentle glow.

He won't hurt me I tell that stubborn wound in my chest.

After the eventful morning, Maxwell decides to forfeit his position in the contest. We go back and forth, but he feels strongly that it's the right thing given what Polly asked him.

After a brief talk with the organizers, he signs a document and the rest will make social media history.

"I can just see the hashtags now. "Banker Baker cashes in his dough."

We both laugh and decide to blow off some steam snowboarding. After a couple of runs down the mountain, I wait at the bottom for Maxwell. It gets dark early this far north and I'm getting cold. We probably missed each other, and he headed back up on the chair lift.

That means it's time to head to the lodge. I warm up by the fire and order us both cups of cider like we had our first night here.

While I scroll the social media fiasco, a resort employee hurries over sans drinks. He whispers a message discretely in my ear. My heart stutters, sinks, and I swallow what feels like cold, cold ice.

I take a shuttle ride to the first aid station, my mind racing ahead in panic. I do something that isn't yogic breathing, huffing and holding, huffing and holding.

"You okay, miss?" the driver asks.

I don't know what I am, but it's not okay.

An ambulance idles outside when we pull up, but the lights aren't on. Oh dear. I rush through the door, bringing in the snow on my boots and concern in my voice when I say, "What happened? Will he be okay?"

Two EMTs dressed in snow gear hover over Maxwell. His right leg is lifted and splinted. "He's stabilized but needs to get to the hospital. Are you his wife?"

Maxwell's eyes rim red with pain when they meet mine. It's from the cold. It can't be that bad, can it?

The EMT says, "He needs emergency care. It could be broken. He has to be checked for spinal damage as well."

Diagnoses and fear blizzard through my mind.

They load him into the ambulance. I never answered the question about whether I'm his wife, but the assumption was there, and his eyes begged me not to disagree. I wouldn't want to be alone right now either.

I want to ask what happened. I want to ask if he's okay. I want to ask what this all means, but I keep my mouth shut and slide my hand into his. It's what I wanted all those years ago. Instead, I was by myself and scared.

After riding along the curving, icy roads, I scurry behind the EMTs as they rush him into the ER. The emergency room personnel disappear with him behind a curtain. I stand there starkly, my hands clasped together, listening as he moans in agony, as voices call commands.

One of the EMTs, a woman in her forties with deep rings beneath her eyes, approaches. "Unfortunately we see accidents like this all the time. I'm sorry. I mean that. It's never easy to see someone you care about in pain." She smiles and claps me on the shoulder and glances at my fingers.

Of course, we're not married. We're not wearing rings. But I don't need to say it.

"I'll keep that to myself," she says with an astute nod at my hand. "But I will share this; he was asking for you. Well, at first he was using combinations of cuss words that would make even the most hardened northerners blush, myself included, but once we had him stabilized, he asked for you, Hazel, right?"

"Yeah."

"Between you and me, his leg will be fine. I'm not a doctor, so don't sue me if I'm wrong, but chances are he'll be up and walking again in six weeks, tops." She wrinkles her nose and shakes her head. "In my non-expert opinion his spine isn't injured, but I'll leave that to the professionals to determine." She winks.

A wave of relief washes over me.

"But that does not mean he won't be without pain. And that

does not mean you can walk away from him in his time of need. You may not be married, but I recommend you stick by him. Understand?"

My eyebrow creeps into an arch as I try to make sense of what she's telling me. "Okay...?" Does she know I'm only now getting used to the idea of being someone's girlfriend?

"If the problem is what I think it is, they'll be calling you in to discuss things in a little while."

A little while turns into three hours as I revisit the humming and beeping unique to hospitals that had been the soundtrack to my own life long ago. I wonder if there's a way to reach Maxwell's family. His phone is back at the cabin. How will we get home? What should I do? Questions circulate in my mind as I sit here, helpless.

Another hour passes. I get a vending machine hot chocolate. It's bitter and watery.

Another hour and I read every tattered magazine in the room.

Yet another hour goes by until finally, a nurse calls, "Mrs. Davis?"

I glance around the room. Oh, me. The pieces of the Styrofoam cup I shredded fall to the floor. I hastily pick them up and follow the nurse down a narrow but brightly lit corridor. Behind the first curtain, there's coughing and hacking. Then there's whining and crying. At last, there's Maxwell, propped up in an adjustable bed with his leg in a plastic air cast.

"The good?" he asks. "You're here."

I take his hand and ask, "The bad?"

"Fracture. Stupid black diamond slope. Ice patch. Ego out of control." His eyes drift and droop with relief, humility, pain medicine, and the awareness that the nurse called *Mrs. Davis*, and I answered, hurrying to his side.

I finally take a breath. They probably kept him waiting so long for test results and more acute patient's needs.

I sit on the edge of the bed and rub the furrows of his palm just like my mom did when I was in the hospital bed after the accident. "No, Maxwell, that's good." It could be so much worse.

He's too bleary on pain medication to ask what I mean or argue.

The nurse brings over a chart and gives me a lengthily rundown of his needs and care. "Every four hours or as needed for pain... Insurance... Primary care... Follow-ups..."

"Thank you," I reply.

"A shuttle from the resort will be here at any moment to transport you back. The EMT arranged it. Be safe," she says, before exiting.

"Now what?" I ask vaguely.

Maxwell's eyes are closed.

What did my mother do for me? Wheelchair, bed, fluids, comfort, encouragement, companionship. I can do that.

Back in the cabin, the fire blazes in the hearth, and a pair of metal warming dishes sit on the table. The first aid center must have communicated with the resort, informing them of our dilemma.

That night, I have the recurring nightmare of the accident that left me wounded so long ago. Waking in twisted sheets and sweat, I witness the transition of the night sky from deep black to dark blue, to faded purple, to gray.

My mind whirs, preventing me from dozing back off. How do we get back to the city? What about after we get back?

This is but one reason I prefer avoiding romantic entanglements. There is too much uncertainty. There are too many feelings. Too wide a margin for error or broken legs.

Maxwell stirs from undisturbed sleep while I provide pain pills, water, and a few slices of toast.

"Are you up for the drive?" he asks.

"Are you?"

"As lovely as this place is, I'd like to get home and see my doctor tomorrow."

"Yeah, sure."

"Keys are in my jacket," he says, pointing.

"I'm driving?" I ask.

"Unless you can fly..."

I'm not sure if that was a joke or if the dosage of pain medication has kicked in because the way he looks at me suggests he sees an angel. I begin to gather up our things. Yes, I can drive, but whether I want to is another matter entirely.

Accelerator, brake, clutch. Blinkers, windshield wipers. We're buckled in. The key is in the ignition, but I'm as frozen as the icicles hanging off the eaves of the lodge.

I'm waiting for Maxwell to say something about getting a move on. He can't be comfortable squished into the passenger seat, even reclined, but we timed his pain management to make the ride as smooth as possible for him.

The sky overhead hangs with dense gray clouds. The ride is under five hours. I've driven along the entire eastern seaboard, during an ill-conceived trip to get out of Manhattan one college spring break when Mother Nature dumped more snow than the streets could handle.

I can do this. I grip the wheel. I turn the key. I'm sliding and then falling into memory.

Yogic breathing. Stay present. Still the mind.

I am safe. I am in control of the car.

The tires crunch over the snow until we reach the main road where the damp cement spits under us. The narrow lane widens and I make a cautious turn toward the highway.

A black SUV with New York plates honks in frustration as I take an agonizingly long time reaching the speed limit. It swerves out from behind me with another blare of its horn. Maxwell remains sedate beside me.

By the time we leave Vermont, gentle flakes drop slowly enough that I count them on the windshield, turning on the wipers when I reach twenty, then thirty flakes. When snow frames the glass, I lean forward. My heart pounds in my throat.

Even though it was decades ago, once more, I see the slide. Feel the loss of control. Butterflies bump in my belly. My father's voice, then my mother waiting for his response before the world went darker than night.

I blink my eyes. "It's a memory, that's all." I exhale.

Should we get off the road? Find somewhere to stay? What if we freeze to death?

I swallow, but my throat is dry.

The defroster blasts white noise instead of music on the stereo like when Maxwell confidently drove us north in a similar storm.

Another SUV blows by us. I follow the glow of red taillights until they disappear. The number of car lengths I can see ahead decreases until the headlights reflect off a white wall of snow.

If we were playing two truths and one lie, the only true thing I could tell Maxwell right now is that I am terrified.

I drop into first gear.

From the passenger seat, Maxwell says, "You can do this." His voice is quiet, comforting, and solid. In his tone, I don't hear him asking me please to get us home safely, he knows I will. He's sharing his reserve of confidence with me. His hand grips mine and then moves to my leg, so I can keep both hands on the wheel, not letting go until the sky gradually opens again and we're back in New York where the snow is merely a sprinkle.

I feel like cheering when the white carpet of the road reveals black asphalt.

I want to pump my arm when billboards and traffic crowd the roadway.

I could kiss the steering wheel when I maneuver into the underground garage and stow the car. Instead, I kiss Maxwell.

"You did well," he says. "I kept my eyes closed because I didn't want to distract you."

"Are you suggesting your eyes are a distraction, Mr. Davis?"

I ask, still strapped into my seatbelt. As soon as the name is out of my mouth, I recall being called Mrs. Davis.

He leans closer. "Ow. My leg. Almost forgot."

"Let's get you upstairs."

Thank goodness for elevators and my own apartment. I feel the need to retreat.

After I get Maxwell settled in, I pop back to my place to shower. Yesterday rushes toward me along with the accident. The two collide. Tears flow freely with the warm water as I come down from the adrenalin of the drive.

When my hair dries, I stand outside Maxwell's door and knock, remembering my first encounter with the Hottie in 7G.

CHAPTER 17
CROSSROADS
MAXWELL

When I was at the bakeoff, and I told Jenna the challenge was a piece of cake, I distinctly recall thinking it couldn't be worse than dealing with Polly Spoonwell earlier that morning. Well, that day got worse and worse in every way except when Hazel said yes to being my girlfriend.

Now, I'm stuck on the couch with a bum leg, helpless to get up when she knocks to check on her hot boyfriend. Not.

I was the guy who'd greet Hazel at the door, muscles flexing as I leaned just so. Instead, because getting up will take a great deal effort, I helplessly yell, "Come in."

The knob jiggles. "Maxwell?" Hazel calls in her lovely British accent.

She appears over the back of the couch and I expect her to dive bomb me with a kiss. She holds back and gives me a little wave. "Are you okay?"

I was about to ask her the same thing. Maybe living in this reality with me is more than she expected when she finally agreed to commit.

Was it too good to be true?

I brush my hand over my face. "I'm sorry, Hazel. I think I

was in denial for most of the ride. I'm sorry you had to look after me last night and drive back here through the storm. It was sweet and brave and—" I give her my best look of apology, but I'm looking like a sorry sack, to begin with. I'd anticipated a fun cap off to our weekend. Not this.

"You would have done the same for me."

I smile in agreement. I'd do anything for her. I'm a guy who dated countless women—even Conrad used to tease that I probably have a black book hiding somewhere. I never denied it. But there is no one I'd rather have play nurse or just hang out with me. She doesn't need to lift a finger. Either way.

As she lingers by the end of the couch, I fear something has shifted between us, but I can't identify what. I think fast. "I'm going to hire help for the next couple of weeks but want to thank you—"

She waves her hands. "There's no need. I'll take care of you."

We go back and forth for a moment—I give her every opportunity to recant her offer. Hazel insists.

I hobble to my feet and give her a spare key and a kiss. We watch reruns of Friends. Recap the disaster that was the baking contest. At midnight, she makes sure I'm comfortable and then goes back to her apartment.

I feel cold and lonely without Hazel here. I want to bake her cookies, woo her, take care of her. I'm helpless. My thoughts seesaw between wanting to give her more and giving up. But that's not who I am.

I grab my phone and send a text. **I wish we were in front of the fire at the cabin**.

The little bubbles blink, indicating she's replying. **Me too**.

I don't know how to tell her I want a future, a real one, a forever one. **I wish you were still here. Goodnight.** I add an emoji heart. I've never been a snuggler before. Then again, I had every reason to believe she wasn't either, but she's really good at it.

I'd like to sleep, but I'm restless because I'm not used to

being stationary for so long. I open my laptop. I have one module left for that silly UUniversity thing. I'll finish it then send a friendly email to my mentees, share the link, and use my current situation as a teaching point for perseverance.

I scan the highlights for the last module. There are reading assignments and journal responses. I read one of the prompts: **Using your journal, free write about what you knew you wanted to be when you were a kid.**

I prickle with resistance but open a fresh document and title it *When I grow up…* The cursor teases me when minutes pass and the page remains blank. I didn't want to be a banker. Not a baker either. I start writing and realize I lean more toward one than the other. Or is my heart leading me to Hazel?

She was the reason I started baking. This program brought me to step out of my comfort zone. To step closer to her.

Could I have both? Or all three? My career, baking, and Hazel. Can I have my cake and eat it too?

I reread the module notes. **Remember the innocence when you were little, how you trusted wholly in yourself, in possibility, and magic. Most of us change as we grow up and our desires take us in different directions. Some of us are told our dreams are impossible. Other times we simply let our dreams go to sleep and fill our lives with what we think is practical, feasible. Visit the attic in your mind and when you dig out those old treasures, hold them in your hand, recall the way your big dreams made you feel.**

What about your dreams in the present? Repeat the exercise above.

This isn't something I can talk to Conrad about or my family. I'm not a put-your-emotions-out-there kind of guy. I remember there was a private online group with the other members of the program. I take a deep breath and then introduce myself using the screen name **BankerBaker**. I instantly regret it because of the hashtags, but it's too late.

I get only a modicum of relief when I agree to the terms—everything shared in the group is confidential.

It looks like a few users are online at this late hour, including TrinaT, NicoleB, and Professor Loves-Her-Life herself. I scroll through the current topic of conversation (pressure from a stubborn and old-fashioned parent). Professor LHL coaches everyone to ask themselves important questions and find answers.

They bare their souls. They write thoughts and feelings and talk to each other through troubles without judgment. I take a risk, introducing myself from the relative anonymity behind the laptop screen.

TrinaT writes: **Anything on your mind tonight?**

I explain what brought me to the program. **It turned out that it helped me try something new, which led me to realize that I could step outside my comfort zone in relationships too, but...**

TrinaT replies: **But...?**

But I'm not sure where this is going.

My fingers hover over the keyboard to say more, but the words to describe my feelings stall between my head and my heart. Then Professor Loves-Her-Life's icon lights up to indicate she's writing.

Professor LHL: **Love doesn't have a roadmap. If it did, no one would get lost.**

My answer comes fast: **I don't feel lost. I know I want to be with her. I'm just nervous. I don't want to do the wrong thing.**

She adds: **Or you're scared...**

I'm not scared either. Okay. Maybe a little. But what if...

What if? All three of them reply.

It's three on one. The words flow this time: **What if she doesn't want to be with me anymore? What if it's too much? What if she leaves me? What if she meets someone else? What if she realizes I'm not the guy for her? What if she wakes up one day, realizes she hates chocolate chip cookies and me and...**

Professor LHL: **The first five, forget. The last one, you're acting nutty.**

Fair enough.

NicoleB: **From my experience, the questions you're asking reveal insecurity, but it's a relatively common, if not normal, part of developing in a relationship. If you were one-hundred percent confident in it, I'd ask for the girl's number and warn her. Trust me, I've been with guys like that and so much ego never turns out well.**

TrinaT: **Exactly what NicoleB said and I'll add that part of having a healthy relationship is communication. You may not want to dump all your insecurities on her, but this might prompt an honest conversation about where you're at and what you'd like in the future. If you're on the same page, great. If not, at least you know.**

I take a moment to let all of this sink in. They're exactly right. The tension in my neck loosens.

Professor LHL writes: **Well said, ladies. Also, when we're feeling stuck, it's because we're thinking about what is or might go wrong in our lives when we should look at what's going right. Now, go deeper. Envision what you might say to her. Think about how it would feel to come out with your concerns. It might draw you closer. She may have the same ones.**

But there's still a part of me, a little voice that tells me to be careful. Not to risk anything.

TrinaT writes: **Have you thought about why you might feel this way? Sometimes exposing old wounds and allowing them to heal will also do the trick.**

In the UUniversity program, they call this process *digging for diamonds in the rough.* My thoughts flit to the engagement ring, the ruined cake, and the proposal that wasn't. I don't dare tell them about that. Likely, I was moving into something serious too soon, especially if we're not rock solid. Caught up in the moment, and afraid of losing her, I acted on a whim. Well, almost.

Professor LHL's avatar lights up then goes dark. Lights up then goes dark. Maybe she's having connectivity issues.

It's like I'm on the edge of knowing something big about myself, but it's still just out of reach...and so is my water bottle. I heave myself to sitting. My leg aches. Like a nor'easter, worries about why Hazel would want to be with me blow into my mind. Why would she want to be with me when I can hardly move?

Professor Loves-Her-Life's avatar lights up again and my computer beeps with a notification when she posts: **Big shifts in our lives take time.**

I slouch on the couch and then reply. **I have plenty of that all of a sudden. I feel like I'm at a crossroads and my compass isn't telling me which direction to go in.**

She writes: **I don't think that's your problem.**

What? That's exactly my problem.

You don't need to read a compass to figure out which direction to take. Love doesn't work like that. You need to follow your heart.

Her comment burns something inside that I can't identify other than feeling a prickle, an irritation, an energy that makes me clench my jaw and ball my hands into fists.

I close my computer without signing off. She doesn't know me, my story, or that my heart did a terrible job guiding me the last time I listened to it. A storm brews inside, winds of war cut across the peaceful calm Professor Loves-Her-Life tried to cultivate. The clouds filling my mind aren't gray, but red.

Anger. Deceit. Distrust.

The truth is that my heart has lied to me in the past.

CHAPTER 18
MEOW
HAZEL

Maxwell is a week into recovery and we're at his doctor's office. Dr. Lee is middle-aged and has a trim beard. I have traumatic flashbacks of months of physical therapy and overhearing doctors whisper their doubts about me ever having the use of my legs again.

After reviewing the most recent X-rays Dr. Lee says, "I think you'll be out of the cast in three weeks."

"Really?" Maxwell asks, lighting up.

"It's healing well, no reason to think otherwise." His expression sharpens. "Stay off it. No activity for another week and then you can move around but just a little. The more gradually you move back into walking, the better chance it has of healing clean. The physical therapists will guide you through strength training."

"The team at the hospital thought more toward eight weeks and talked about surgery..." Maxwell says, not quite believing the news.

"They were being cautious. She's been taking good care of you," the doctor says with a smile in my direction. "You're a very lucky man."

"I am," Maxwell agrees.

We go to another office in the same building and Maxwell meets with the physical therapist. He leaves with a piece of paper outlining a few simple exercises to do at home to maintain muscle tone and circulation.

When we return to our building, a box waits for me in front of my door. Leaning heavily on his crutches, Maxwell waits in his doorway and says, "Ooh, do you have a secret admirer?"

I cast him a smirk. "Several."

He's somehow still attractive with an air cast on his leg, joggers, a hoodie, and waiting for me to open the parcel.

"Go ahead, I won't be jealous."

I pull out a pair of shiny black high heels with red soles. They look like they'll knock someone's socks off. A little note says *For when I can walk again. XO Maxwell*

I ignore the XO part for now and beam a smile. "How did you know I wanted these?"

"I saw you browsing them on your phone."

"I love them," I say, clutching the shoes to my chest.

His smile is sleepy. "I'm going to rest. But when I'm back on my feet, I'd like to take you on a proper date."

"I'll be over tonight after my class to help you with your exercises."

"And dinner?"

I nod. "Dessert?"

Maxwell stares forlornly in the direction of the kitchen.

"My friend Omar is a personal trainer. Maybe he can come over to help—" Though I know as well as the professionals that healing happens in its own time.

Maxwell shakes his head. "It's not that."

"Are you restless?"

His shoulder rises and falls without comment. He seems deep in thought so I don't press him. He hasn't baked since we were in Vermont. Maybe it was his way of blowing off steam. Then again, it was a relatively new hobby.

Is this how domestication begins? Remember my theory

about swans, peacocks, and pigeons? Well, peahens. I'm used to spreading my wings, but I'm afraid I'll just fly right into Maxwell's arms. Plus, peahens don't wear shoes like this.

By the end of the week, like a champ, Maxwell crushes the exercises the physical therapist suggested: leg lifts, extensions, and gentle resistance. When we're done with our third round, he scrubs his face with his hands. Healing isn't easy.

As the week progress, he even makes it over to my apartment a few times for a change of scenery.

Early one morning my phone beeps with a text while I'm brushing my teeth. **Come Quick.** Without stopping or spitting the toothpaste foam into the sink, I hurry to 7G, worried he took a spill or started a fire and can't get to the extinguisher.

He's standing at his bathroom vanity casually brushing his teeth. I slowly resume doing the same, not sure why he rang the alarm bell.

Our brushes *shush* in time. Otherwise, the room is silent.

Awareness returns. I'm standing here with bedhead hair in a messy bun, an old sweatshirt, and leggings stained with paint. I'm not a vision of early morning beauty.

I grip the flecked marble counter, stabilizing myself. I don't know what to do with the spit. Why didn't I leave my toothbrush at home? I can't ask what Maxwell wanted because my mouth is full. I avoid meeting his eyes because I don't want either of us to acknowledge the frothy paste breaching my lips as I scrub my teeth.

There's a second bathroom, but he'll think it's strange if I suddenly run in there, and is likely to hobble after me, tripping on the laundry overflowing from the basket.

Frozen, like a scared rabbit, but not feeling at all bright-eyed and bushy-tailed, I realize I've been brushing my teeth for a full three minutes now. My dentist would be proud.

Maxwell washes his face, patting dry the shadow of stubble along his jawline. "You're just in time."

I rapidly shake my head and ask him what the emergency was, but he can't understand me.

He points at the sink.

I shake my head.

I don't even think my father ever saw me brush my teeth. It's mortifying, humiliating, and so foamy! He must sense my deer-in-the-headlights fear.

"You okay?" Maxwell says casually.

I whimper. I want to ask him the same question regarding the text but cannot. I spin my finger in a circle to indicate he turn around.

His eyes narrow in question.

I mumble an unintelligible, "Don't look."

He covers his eyes, but as soon as the white foam funnels from my mouth that sly fox peeks.

My cheeks blister along with my shoulders, my outie, and my kneecaps. Full body embarrassment.

I wipe my face and then say, "Obviously, there's no emergency. Get *meow*tta here." I run from the room only to stop short when I catch a whiff of something sweet coming from the kitchen. How did I miss that before? Oh, right. Minty freshness filled my nostrils.

Maxwell pads across the room with an uneven gait. "Yeah, I wanted you to get breakfast straight from the oven. Wait. Did you just say *meow*?"

"I have no idea what you're talking a*meow*t." Fluttery panic makes me flap around.

Maxwell's brow furrows. "I'm pretty sure you just did it again."

"I don't know what you're *meow*n."

"*Meow*?" Maxwell asks.

In the stark daylight filtering in from the slatted blinds, his smile reveals perplexed amusement. His dark lashes skim his cheeks. His hair is tousled. His chin is a masterpiece. This man is too handsome for my own good.

My heart thuds between us. "I need a *meow*ment."

This is getting intense. Maybe I need to follow my own advice. I might be falling...no, I already did. But I'm afraid of where I'm going to land. But there aren't maps for this kind of thing, right?

It's like my internal GPS repeats *Destination unknown. Recalculating.*

My feet slap the hardwood floor as I make a break for the door. "I need coffee. Want anything?"

"I have coffee and I'm heating up a jumbo chocolate, pecan cinnamon roll with spiced drizzle. The bakery on 74th delivers. That's why I wanted you to come over." Maxwell thumbs in the direction of the kitchen. "Any day now, I'll be back in there wearing my apron and you'll never want to leave."

If I've resorted to speaking *meow*, that means I'm a cat and I need my independence. *Meow*. Now. Immediately.

My worlds have collided. Maxwell is serious about us. But am I?

I dash down the hall, pound the button for the lobby in the elevator, and inhale deeply when I reach the street. Like a cat on the side of a thunderous path, I bob and weave amidst the oncoming traffic. An irritable honk from a cabbie startles me and I dodge a paper bag caught in the wind. I sprint five blocks, ten, putting as much distance as I can between our building and me. I only slow when I remember my excuse: coffee. Starbucks supplies me with a macchiato.

I drift along the streets as the day warms with a hint of the spring thaw. Icicles drip, slush runs in puddles along the sides of the road. I pass a park revealing the green of crocus shoots and tender grass. Boutiques advertise winter sales and clearance shopping. Office buildings and restaurants crowd with people glad to be outdoors. I rarely see this much city in such a short amount of time. I wander until I smell chocolate and butter—a bakery on the corner invites me in. I order a cookie.

It's fresh and chocolate chip and as big as my head. I break it in half and shove it in my mouth like a starved animal. Crumbs dot my jacket. It doesn't matter; I've crossed the line of composure and mystery. Maxwell saw me brushing my teeth. I'm ruined! I tuck the other half of the cookie back into the wax bag. My phone vibrates with a few texts—one from Catherine, another from Lottie, but notably none from Maxwell.

I ignore them because I can only think about him. Later, my phone rings with a call from the studio, wondering why I didn't show up to teach. Why? Because I brushed my teeth in front of a guy, leaving me feeling vulnerable and confused and senseless. I scrub my hands down my face. I forgot to go to work. Seriously this time, what's happening to me?

I continue to roam Manhattan until the sun dips behind the skyscrapers and the commuters leave work for a weekend spent relaxing or out on the town.

Since meeting Maxwell, I lost track of Hazel, the empowered, independent female. I'm on a mission to find her.

I take a cab back to my neighborhood and creep past his door. I wash away the city grime. I scrub and exfoliate. I moisturize and primp, returning to my effortlessly put-together self. I pull on my tightest dress. I try on the heels Maxwell gave me, but I don't need reminders of him with me tonight and trade them for a different pair.

I call up my girlfriends, leaving them messages to meet me later. I send a dozen texts with the address of the club I'm going to. But when I get there, bypassing the line and instantly engulfed in the party vibe of vices and victory over monogamy, I don't see any familiar faces. Is the turnover that quick in this city? Out of the game for a few weeks and I don't recognize anyone?

I get a reply from Lottie. **On a date. Let's meet for brunch tomorrow!**

A message comes in from Tyler. **Busy, babe. Let's grab coffee soon.**

Then Minnie writes. **Broadway show and a late dinner with a friend ;-)**

No, I want to dance and forget about couples and commitment. I don't want to think about Maxwell. He doesn't call or text, but that doesn't make it easier. A man wearing a V-neck T-shirt leans close to my ear, trying to talk, but I can't hear him over the music.

"Get *meow*tta here," I mutter and rush off, regretting going out. My old life no longer fits.

Once again, I creep past Maxwell's door. Floral perfume and the vague scent of baking cookies waft in the hallway. A twinge in my belly turns into a stab in my gut, leaving me more confused than ever.

CHAPTER 19
BLONDIE
MAXWELL

While I get ready to stay home again the next morning, I keep an ear on the hallway, listening for the telltale sounds of Hazel leaving her apartment.

I don't understand why she wouldn't brush her teeth in front of me. It's not that weird. Why'd she flee? It's been less than a day and I already miss hanging out with her. Also, I can't quite fluff my pillows the same way she can with one on my side and another under my knee.

A long sigh escapes. We're not married. It isn't like she has to answer to me. I was going to text, but my phone battery died and the cord was in the other room. I'm getting around better now, but I figured she'd be right back. Now, I wonder if she needs her space.

What needs to happen is I need to get back on track. I've kept up with work to a degree but miss going into the office. I miss baking. I miss Hazel.

Just then the door whooshes open and in walks a sight for sore eyes.

"Hello," the tall, leggy blond says. The rough edges to her movements suggest she's upset. No, beyond upset. Furious. She tosses her hair and her nostrils flare.

"Don't you dare call me Blondie, either. You're on thin ice, Maxwell."

I look behind Blondie to see if she brought the rest of the battalion, but she's marched in here solo. My gaze lingers on Hazel's door then flits in the other direction to the elevator. I think I hear laughter. It could be the TV or maybe I'm just over-tired and overthinking things.

Hazel is a free woman. She can do what she wants.

"What happened to you?" Blondie asks.

"Hazelnut."

The returned expression is not one of amusement. "What? No games, Maxwell. I want the full story."

"Come with me to my physical therapy appointment and if you promise not to bite my head off, I'll tell you everything."

The cab ride isn't long enough for me to get out the full story, just disjointed pieces that do nothing to plead my case. When Blondie gets ticked off, watch out world.

When I check-in for my appointment, the PT assistant informs me I'm trying something different today—a group class. "It's a new program. A lot of times, people in physical therapy are homebound for the most part. It can get lonely, so we're testing out a general movement class that incorporates a social hour."

"You're welcome to join him, Mrs. Davis."

I burst into laughter. "You can call her Blondie."

That gets me a wrap on the back of my head.

Nonetheless, she follows me to a large room with eight chairs filled with five silver-haired people and a male physical therapist named Scotty who I've only ever seen wear shorts.

We begin with gentle stretching from the chair—Scotty tells us to do these twice a day at home to improve circulation.

The five older folks regale us with stories about their health, the good old days, war stories—both on the battlefield and on the homefront. A woman named Peggy tries to give Blondie a quiche recipe.

"I'm the better candidate for baked goods," I interject.

Blondie looks at me like I have two heads. Meanwhile, Maria, seated beside me, proudly shares photos of her twenty-one grandchildren. It's all very endearing and sweet.

My wallet falls out of my pocket and Blondie and I bump heads when we try to pick it up. We exchange a look. One easily mistaken for an expression of endearment.

In reality, it's more like warning shots.

Her: *Watch where you're swinging that thing, Fat Head.*

Me: *Don't you dare say anything about my large head, Blondie. Takes one to know one.*

Her: *If you call me Blondie one more time, I'm going to tear your head off.*

Me: *I'd like to see you try.*

Of course, this is all a silent war of words.

Maud, a woman who reminds me of our grandmother, blurts, "Ah, to be young and in love. When you reach our age, every experience is intimate. How can it not be? We're so close to life and death. It would be a shame to miss out on any of it because you just never know when—"

"When your number will be up." Ralph, Maud's crotchety old husband, finishes for her. "Any day now, any day," he mumbles.

She continues more delicately, "I don't mean for it to sound morbid. Of course, by intimacy, I mean being close to every moment and to each other."

Blondie waves her hands. "No, we're not—"

Scotty interrupts a potentially embarrassing moment and tells us to get to our feet, hold the chair for stability, and do leg lifts.

I'm used to going to the gym every day, but this is tedious. Thankfully, Scotty wraps things up and says, "I'll see you all next week."

"You might not," an older, crotchety man says. "There's the diabetes, the stent in my heart, the herniated disc, the recurring gout, risk of pneumonia, a piano could fall from a window...I could go at any minute."

"Walter!" Maria scolds.

"What? I'm ninety-six; it's a miracle I'm still breathing."

I look at Blondie, get a flash of what she'll look like in fifty years, and glimpse what the wrinkly, white-haired people used to look like. Something softens inside. They're old but distinguished. They earned the lines on their faces. And I realize, I want that. All of it. With Hazel. I don't want to grow old alone or be bitter.

During the time spent hanging out with Hazel, our weekend away, my failed proposal, UUniversity, and now my recovery each bring me a step closer to giving myself fully over to a relationship with her, but there's still a distance to go.

On the cab ride back, Blondie says, "What has gotten into you?"

"I started to tell you."

"Okay. I'm listening. But give me the Cliffsnotes."

"As you know, I switched majors four times before I settled on finance. Up until my current apartment, I never stayed in the same one for more than a year or so. I never dated the same woman more than a couple of times. Am I the kind of guy who goes to the same restaurant two nights in a row? No. Like a rock climber, I'm always anticipating the next hand or foothold. You could say I have a hard time picking and sticking with something or someone."

Blondie cackles because it's true.

I sigh.

Then she says, "But you've found the one and you're scared. Oh, Fat Head. You are your own worst enemy."

"No, that's you Blondie."

She socks me in the arm. It hurts just as much as it did when we were kids even though I'm twice her size now.

When we reach my building, I'm pretty sure Hazel slips around the corner and dashes into her apartment as we exit the elevator. By now, Blondie and I are laughing about old times. She's still irritated with me, but that's nothing new.

I'm pretty sure Hazel is avoiding me, and I'm not sure why. Unless she's experiencing the same thing as me. Uncertainty. Trepidation.

Blondie calls me a pencil-in kind of guy. As in, I won't use a pen in case I have a change of plans so a pencil it is. But when it comes to Hazel, I want to use a permanent marker.

After three days of my houseguest and not seeing Hazel, I am ready to run, even if it means reinjuring my leg. Maybe she's out of town. Maybe I could trade Blondie for her.

All I can think about are Hazel's long legs, her intelligent thoughts, and her bright smile. Also, her lips. I'd be a liar if I denied that.

If I can't have her, I can have sugar. I make Blondie a batch of blondies. Well, three, until I land on the right balance of butter and sugar. I don't want them dry or oily. I also tell her my plan for the ring, but she's not so sure it's a wise idea given Hazel's absence.

While putting away the dishes, I hear a faint sound. I follow it to the hallway. Mew *meows* at the door. Hazel's cat rubs against the doorframe.

"What are you doing here?" My gaze flies to her door, but it's closed. "You've never even been outside."

The last five texts I've sent Hazel remain unopened. Maybe she lost her phone...and her cat. I send a text. Then a cookie emoji. Then a cat head.

When she doesn't reply, I call.

When she doesn't answer, I knock on our shared wall.

"Are you home?"

Silence.

"I have Mew." I bite my lip. "Meow?" Maybe that'll get her to respond.

Instead, the actual cat and Blondie give me a deep side-eye.

I head to the hall and her door opens a sliver.

The look she gives me says everything she doesn't. Or can't.

I miss you.

"I have something for you. Would you mind coming over for a minute?" I ask.

Blondie waits by the front door. Her smile is forced.

I silently scold her with a scowl. "Hazel, meet Blondie. Blondie, this is Hazel."

She glares at me and extends her slender hand. "I'm Audrey."

I grunt.

Hazel looks like she wants to shrink or shank someone.

"I'm Maxwell's sister," she clarifies.

Hazel's eyes widen. "Oh. I thought. Never mind. Nice to meet you."

Her smile hides her sister-bear protection. "Likewise. Finally."

"Finally?" she asks.

Blondie throws her thumb in my direction. "He wanted us to meet before I go home."

"Have you enjoyed your visit?"

"I was here on business but found my brother alone on the couch, with a broken ankle and a broken—"

My voice is stiff when I cut her off. "It's not broken," I mutter then paste on a smile. "Nothing like having family around. I made some cookies and blondies," I add sharply.

"And that's about all, aside from watching Friends repeats," Audrey says drily.

"Hey, I've been working too."

"Well, I should go pack and leave you two to your cookies and milk," Audrey says.

When the door to the spare room closes I say, "Sorry. She's protective."

"Of who?" Hazel asks, "Because it sounded like she was scolding us both."

"She's a high achiever and likes things just so. She doesn't understand how things can fall apart because she's so good at keeping them together. I guess I have a hard time with that too."

"Is she married?" Hazel asks.

"Happily. Four kids. And a career. One of those superwomen who do it all. Our parents are very proud. Trust me though, she knows how to delegate."

We stand at opposite ends of the hall. The entrance to the kitchen emits a sweet, chocolate aroma that seems to grow and glow between us like a living thing and not a plate of little round disks dotted with chocolate.

"I baked to prove that I'm not a complete klutz in the kitchen —and because I'm slightly addicted. I once caught the oven on fire back home so I had some remedial work to do."

Hazel's smile lights up the dim hall. "You've come a long way."

I shrug. "I'm a klutz at other things too."

"The snowboarding injury was an accident." Hazel's British accent goes wobbly. "Could have happened to anyone."

Our eyes meet.

Just then, the door opens and Audrey rolls out her suitcase.

"Well, glad I'm leaving my brother in good hands. Call me if you need anything."

"Okay, Mom," I say, hugging her.

"If Mom knew you were down here alone, with a broken leg—"

"It's not broken and I'm not alone." To Hazel, I say, "The women in my family can be a little overbearing."

"We care, Fat Head," Audrey says, but her tone is less prickly.

"I know," I say. "Tell everyone at home I say hi. Give each of those kids a hug from Uncle Max and one for your hubby while you're at it. I imagine he misses you." I'm not sure if I'm joking or not.

"Of course. I'll be back in June to finish this merger. Hallelujah."

She brushes past Hazel on her way to the door. "If what Maxwell said is true, then I hope to see you again."

My pulse quickens as the door closes.

I don't want her to scare Hazel off again. She might need distance and boundaries. She might want something casual. I don't know.

We each examine the corners of the hall, the molding, the carpet fibers, all the details between us until the elevator dings. When I glance up, she's looking at me.

"She seems—" Hazel bites her lip. "Fat Head?"

"Never repeat it. The Davis family have large heads. More brains. More smarts."

Hazel chuckles. "Just keep telling yourself that."

"Do you want—?" I point toward the kitchen.

Hazel doesn't move. "You didn't tell your mother about your ankle?"

"She worries too much and her blood pressure—" What about my blood pressure because right now I feel every beat of my pulse. "A cookie?" I ask, finishing my sentence from before and limping into the kitchen.

Hazel shakes her head slowly as if apprehensive. One cookie could lead to another. Two cookies could lead to a kiss...

CHAPTER 20
MUSHY MARSHMALLOW
HAZEL

I've mentioned a lot of nevers. I've never taken a trip with a guy before. I've never been in love. I never get the same coffee two days in a row. I've also never kissed the same guy twice...or more than twice. I've lost count now. So it's probably best I keep my distance from Maxwell.

Easier said than done. His apartment smells like spicy soap, winter, and chocolate. The stainless steel appliances and the dark wood and marble of the kitchen remind me of how easily I succumbed to cookies...to him.

His buttery soft cotton T-shirt shifts when he moves toward me, revealing irresistible muscles. Everything about him is perfect. Too perfect.

"Listen, Hazel, I'm confused. You've been avoiding me. Is something on your mind?" he blurts.

"This is going fast. I thought it was casual. But it's not, not at all." Heat rises to my cheeks. The dam holding back the river of emotion I have for him strains against the torrent.

"And that's a problem, why?"

The words to explain rise to my lips, but it's too risky. I saw what happened to my mother. It's better to end things before I end up like her. "I can't do this. You don't understand. I want you to leave me alone." I reinforce the dam with those words. Words that hurt to speak. My voice is surprisingly small.

Maxwell swallows hard. "If that's what you want."

"I should go."

"You should stay." He reaches for me.

I look up, wishing we could start over or that we were different people, meeting for the first time. He licks his lip. I bite my bottom one. There is no denying the electricity between us. But that's just it. We're going to get hurt if we continue. That's the only possible outcome. I've seen it play out in real life.

"Goodbye, Maxwell," I fire because, in the game of chess, we'll even sacrifice ourselves to get what we think we want.

Sometimes words, the flat panel of a turned back, and a goodbye are the fiercest weapons we have.

When I get back to the apartment, I open my laptop, prepared to help others. That usually quells the ache inside.

Only, my last conversation was with program member BakerBanker.

I instantly knew it was Maxwell. How he ended up in my program is beyond me. My chest craters. He wants something that I can't give him.

A week passes.

A horrible, lonely, melancholy week. I get stuck in a yoga pose, burst into tears at the scent of cake as I pass a bakery, and read half of Catherine's book collection.

It's Saturday night. I should be out and having fun. The only way to leave the building, aside from the fire escape, is by walking past Maxwell's door. I give myself a pep talk. I'll strut by, doing my best power walk like the strong, independent woman I am.

I don't move.

The walls and borders between Maxwell and I remain erect. Maybe I should have a party. I call Lottie, Tyler, Colette, Minnie, and Harry. I tell them to invite friends—the more the merrier. I stock up on drinks and snacks. When I return to the apartment, I put on music and remind Mew to be a friendly host.

As everyone filters in, someone turns up the music and the conversation gets even louder. The last time we gathered here was for our Galentine's Day party when Maxwell stopped by.

I eye the door, half expecting him to sidle in.

Even though the living room is full of friends and laughter, it somehow feels empty. I feel empty.

Better now than later, that little voice tells me. Strangely, she sounds a lot like my mother.

We talk about Tyler's next trip to France, Catherine gallivanting around Italy, and how Colette wants to visit Belgium. Lottie's contribution is copious amounts of laughter and a reminder of the time as she repeatedly checks her phone. After we're all giggling about college days, work mishaps, and Minnie's trouble with her neighbor—tell me about it—I'm reminded of old times.

Only, now, I'm different. Instead of regaling them with stories of my many dates, only one guy springs to mind. And stays there.

"What brought on the Belgian fixation?" Lottie asks Colette after she brings it up for the third time.

"Was it a guy?" Minnie follows up.

There's chatter about the latest in their love lives.

"What about you?" Colette asks me. "You have that certain glow."

"I've been doing a lot of yoga," I mumble.

Lottie asks, "You went out last weekend, right?"

"Oh, um."

"Oh, um?" she repeats.

I shake my head.

Just then, there's a knock on the door. Expecting more guests, or Harry at least, I swing it open without thinking to look through the peephole. Maxwell stands there and asks, "Why didn't I get an invitation? You know I'm the best baker on the block." He smiles, fully jesting, and balancing on his air cast and holding a platter of tartlets topped with berries and cream.

I break out into a sweat everywhere: my hands, my feet, my neck, my hairline. Have I mentioned I never get ruffled? Well, his unexpected pop-in, or rather pop-over, rattles me. It unhinges me. My cheeks match the tiny bows on Minnie's shirt.

Lottie appears at my side, giving us both a long once over. "I didn't realize you were expecting anyone else."

"I told you to invite friends."

"We're not enough?" Tyler teases.

They all remember Maxwell and welcome him in, not realizing the boundary I created. Not knowing about anything that's gone on in the last month because I kept it to myself.

Maxwell and Tyler each get a helping of nachos and chat about the ankle injury.

"Hazel, you didn't mention you took a ski trip. Why wasn't I invited?" Tyler pouts.

"It was a work thing."

Maxwell shrugs. "Mixture of business and pleasure."

"How is UUniversity going, anyway? I saw an ad for it on social the other day," Colette says.

My stomach cartwheels.

"Yeah, it seems pretty cool. You should open a center where people can meet in-person. You can teach yoga, you could—" Tyler starts.

"You should close your mouth," I mutter so softly no one else hears me.

Maxwell gives me a sharp and surprised look.

I steal a corn chip covered with cheese from Maxwell's plate and stuff it in my mouth.

Lottie helps herself to another raspberry lime sparkling water and keeps checking her phone.

"Expecting a call? A text?" Tyler asks.

Colette's eyes flash in Maxwell and my direction. "A text. A phone number…A contact. That's him! The one that when you think about you get all mushy inside," she exclaims as though she just solved a whodunit.

"The Galentine guy!" Lottie says, making the connection.

"He was here all along," Minnie says.

Everyone watches me, including Maxwell.

"It's after nine." I gesture to the door.

Mew scolds me with narrowed cat-eyes.

"Since when is that late to you?" Tyler asks.

"I have to get up early to teach a class," I answer. Early being eleven tomorrow morning.

"I should go anyway." Colette gets to her feet and glances at her phone again.

There's a round of *oohs*.

"He gets off work now. Thanks guys." Colette dashes out the door.

Lottie whispers, "She's head over heels for this guy. They've been spending tons of time together, but she's afraid it's moving too fast. When his visa expires..."

"Nothing wrong with fast," Tyler says. "If you're into it, you're into it. No need to try to control the rate of speed."

"But she wants to be careful," Minnie says pointedly.

I wonder if they're speaking in code to each other.

I feel Maxwell's eyes on me. In fact, they've hardly left me all night. I'm all mushy inside, outside, all over.

"No, she's afraid of falling in love," Lottie says dramatically.

"Look what happened last time," I say.

Maxwell asks, "What happened?"

"Left at the altar."

"So sad," Lottie. "On that note, I should head out too. I have to work in the morning."

That leaves Tyler, Minnie, Maxwell, and me.

Tyler's knowing eyes flit between us then land on Minnie. They say goodnight and leave together.

Then it's just Maxwell and me.

I interrupt the silence with clinking glasses and plates as I clean up. He grabs the hem of my sleeve, halting me in my tracks. "Come here." His words tickle me. "What's this about me making you mushy."

"You were there. It's no big deal. That was last month. It's not like I'm still mushy."

"I think you're mushier than ever." His not-quite brown eyes tease me.

"Mew, should I be offended?" I ask as the cat stalks into the room.

"And UUniversity. Care to comment about that?"

I shake my head.

"Hazelnut." His voice is stern.

"Maxie."

"I took a risk baking cookies that time. I took a risk, taking that online class. I took a risk coming over here tonight. I want to take a risk on us. But if that truly isn't what you want—" Maxwell's face begins to crumble when I don't reply. He pulls back.

"I need to think. As I said, I need space."

He gives me a gentle kiss on the cheek in reply.

I want to lean in. I want him to hold me. I want to hear that this is going to work out.

But I know well enough that there aren't guarantees. I could end up just like my mother.

"I'll be here," he says. "Or rather, there." Then he limps to the door and with a brief glance over his shoulder, he exits.

Mew glares at me, sticks his nose in the air, and retreats down the hall.

I don't blame him.

The same what-ifs Maxwell mentioned in his UUniversity posts torment me. My own advice shouts loudly in my ears.

It's not that easy though.

The fear of rejection is strong. I don't want to be like my mother—duped and left never knowing if my father was remorseful for what he did.

I'm more confused than ever.

I've never given a full-hearted yes to much of anything in my life. I've never committed—not to jobs, apartments, cities, or guys. But what-if?

Another voice joins in the cacophony. What if it does work out? What if I experience lifelong happiness? I mean, I'm not so naïve to think there won't be ups and downs, but the what-ifs work both ways. Right?

And yet, that stubborn voice in my head puts its foot down, demanding I protect my heart at all costs. And the foot is slender, has a pedicure, and closely resembles my mother's.

My chest is heavy, aches. I slouch into bed even though it's relatively early by weekend-in-the-city standards. Laughter and cars filter from the street below. This apartment has high ceilings, a modern, neutral palette, a city vista of twinkling lights, and the river far off in the distance.

But I'm alone.

This can't be all there is.

The thought that I have to protect my heart at all costs weighs on me. It already hurts. The pain is from pushing Maxwell away. From his absence. So how is this protecting my heart?

Instead of the voices in my head, I listen to the building's noises, the creek of the floor overhead, the intermittent honking outside.

Picking up one of Catherine's romance novels, I start reading.

The main character in *Sweetie Pies and Queen Bees* makes bad decision after lousy choice. She has me frustrated and disappointed and more than once, I want to throw the book across the room or sit her down and talk some sense into her.

The guy loves her. She loves him. What's the problem?

I continue reading then tear myself away from the page, not trusting the happily ever after, and log onto my computer.

In the private UUniversity group, I confess that I care about a guy, a lot. **But fear is holding me back. Overwhelm. What-ifs.**

TrinaT is on most nights. She writes: **We were talking about this recently. What if things go right? Didn't you say to focus on that?**

She's got me there. A sigh flutters out of me. I managed to excel in loving my life. This program is a case in point. But my love life? That's another story.

Then the avatar for the BankerBaker lights up. **Yeah, what about the guy who adores you? Who's willing to do anything to make this work? To prove himself worthy. Who learned to bake because he fell in love with the girl next door but was too immature to tell her outright so he tried to lure her by wafting the sweet scent of chocolate her way?**

Oh wow.

I feel a tug. Longing. A craving.

I only have one solution.

Cookies.

CHAPTER 21
ONE STEP AT A TIME
MAXWELL

Rarely in life have I felt lost. But without Hazel, my inner compass spins wildly. Then again, I'm not going anywhere fast with this air cast.

I'd hoped by showing up at her gathering, we could pick up where we'd left off. But I'm not sure where that is anymore. She says she doesn't want to be with me, but the look in her eyes, the lean toward me, everything about her appearance tells me a different story, lighting hope in my heart.

But I'll respect her wishes even if I don't understand them.

UUniversity gave me an outline for a possible future and provided a roadmap. Maybe it'll show me how to find my way forward...or lead me to Hazel. Her friends mentioned she was somehow associated with UUniversity. Maybe another student? Administrator. What would her username be? *Hazelnut*. No, that's my nickname for her. Something to do with ballet, yoga, or hiking? Those are among her many interests.

I log on.

NicoleB writes: **Where've you been? How'd everything work out?**

Professor Loves-Her-Life posts a quandary about a guy and what-ifs and things going right.

Am I going hazel*nuts*?

I blink a few times. She's into yoga and self-improvement. I recall her mentioning she developed an app a while back. Made bank. Maybe this is her most recent endeavor?

Is Hazel Professor LHL? I'm about to knock on her door but hold back. She didn't trick me on purpose, but I feel duped. Confused.

I consider calling Conrad. He'd tell me to man up.

I consider calling my sister. She'd tell me to leave her alone.

My parents? They'd start planning the wedding.

No. I can handle this.

They're just feelings.

I really need to get back to the gym.

I know what I want but am used to getting my way.

The answer comes as the cursor blinks. Patience. Prayer.

The others chime in, telling Professor LHL to go for it. Telling me to give my mystery woman time, assuring me that if it's meant to be she'll come around.

They have no idea I'm talking about Hazel and unless I actually am crazy, she's talking about me. This buoys me. I could run around the block right now.

Then Professor LHL types: **The hardest part might be the craving. See, I love chocolate chip cookies. I have the recipe, but they're not the same. He makes them better**.

TrinaT writes: **Are you using him for his baking abilities?**

Then Nicole posts about a dozen exclamation points. She figured it out.

It's not a huge stretch given my username BankerBaker.

TrinaT: **It's you two, isn't it!**

Guilty.

NicoleB: **Professor, with all due respect, there's some proverb about teaching what you need to learn, but you also have to practice what you preach. Go give the poor guy a chance. Worst case, it doesn't work out. Best case, it does and you live happily ever after.**

Moments later, someone knocks on the door, and the key slides into the lock. She knows I'm not quick on my feet at the moment. But it's as though the key slides into my heart. It bursts with hope.

Hazel stands in the doorway with her hair piled on top of her head. She wears a cozy sweater, leggings, and fuzzy slippers. "Like NicoleB wrote, worst case it doesn't work out between us. That's what I'm afraid of."

"She also said best case, it does and we live happily ever after."

"That's just it. I know it won't work out."

I frown. "Evidence please because that goes against what you teach in UUniversity."

She draws a deep breath. "I started the program as a form of life coaching. It's easier to help people all day and night with their problems, goals, and dreams. But I've been on the hot mess express for years. I am not the chief executive officer of my life. I'm a big failure. A fake."

"You've helped loads of people. You helped me. You're not a failure or a fake. You just need to listen to your own advice. Walk the talk and all that."

I rub her shoulder and then she moves in for a hug.

Through the tears dampening my fleece, she says, "How? How does a person get over the pain of the past?"

I hold her steady. "I don't know what happened to you, but I do know you heal one step at a time. Sometimes literally." I give my boot a shake to lighten the moment.

She half-giggles. "I just don't always make it easy for myself. I get in my own way, overthinking and analyzing things."

"You have a community of women ready to help you. You have me."

She tips her head up to meet my eyes.

"I came to UUniversity when I was feeling stuck—I'd achieved those big dreams that everyone is supposed to have. I had them but something was still missing. You."

Her eyes brim, but she holds back tears.

"Confession: I didn't do all of the modules. I didn't participate in all of the tasks. But it gave me the confidence to branch out beyond my comfort zone...mainly because my comfort zone was no longer comfortable. I think you've created a comfort zone but might feel the same. Something is missing."

"Or someone," she says. "I found him. That's what scares me."

The sadness in her eyes dims the candle of hope within.

"I've never told anyone this. Not even Catherine." Her voice is scratchy, but she continues anyway. "When I was little, I caught my father cheating on my mom."

My stomach twists and I reach for her hand. I'm the guy that leaves the room or the movie theater during cheating scenes. I can't stomach it.

"I never told anyone because when he spotted me catching them, he gave a subtle shake of his head and mouthed, *No one will believe you.*"

"And you've spent the rest of your life proving yourself?" I whisper.

A dry laugh escapes Hazel's lips. "You should run UUniversity. That's exactly it. I've proved myself in every other possible way...and kept my distance from men. One date and done. I never give them a chance to cheat which has also meant I never gave myself a chance to fall in love. Until now."

The candle blazes. I keep my cool though. "You think I should be a life coach?" I shake my head and wrap my arms around Hazel. "I'm better suited to banking and baking. But I'm so sorry about all that with your father and how you've kept it with you all this time."

"The thing is, my mother knew. They stayed married for appearances—their money and social lives were enmeshed. He took his secret to the grave."

"But you said your mom knew."

"She was too proud to admit it. But I could tell. When he'd

go on business trips—that's when we'd do things like move and make crazy-roni—I'd hear her crying at night. She told me, 'Never trust a man with something as precious as your heart.' And I never have."

The words *until now* echo. I say, "You're intelligent and beautiful and courageous—"

She playfully whacks me. "Oh, come on, you're going to give me a big head."

"No, I'm the fat head. Remember, Audrey? But joking aside, you're also strong. I think your heart is stronger than you're giving it credit for. And I happen to know that I'm not the kind of guy that would do anything to hurt you like cheating." I scrub my hand on the back of my neck.

"You can't make that promise," she says sharply.

"I can. You know how we're birds of a feather? In college, I met a girl. We fell for each other hard and fast. I thought she was the one. Turned out I was one...of three. She was dating three guys. Now, when I say we were dating, it wasn't casual dinners out. We were planning our future. She met my family. We spent the holidays together. This went on for three years. Her roommate exposed her. It was like an intervention. All of us guys showed up together, completely confused. Humiliated. I got punched in the gut. The other guy got knocked in the jaw. We each thought the other man had our woman."

"She was playing all of you."

"Sure was. Like a fiddle. Like a race to see who'd be the most successful. Then she'd ditch the other two and go ahead and marry the victor."

"That's incredibly clever...and devious. I'm sorry Maxwell."

"Yes, we were young, but as you said, our lives were enmeshed. It crushed me. I told myself I'd never, ever get serious with someone again." I hobble over to a drawer and pull out a little black book. Slapping it on the table I say, "Evidence that I kept my word to myself."

Her eyes widen. The book is thick.

"Until you. Everything changed. I will keep my word to you. I will never cheat on you. I may forget to run an errand or miss a special occasion or not get how you like the towels folded right, but I will be true to you, Hazel."

Liquid drips from her eyes.

"I say this from the most loving place, but all that stuff that happened with your dad, that was a long, long time ago now. You're not your mother. I'm not your father." I pause. "That would be weird. But I think you know what I mean."

"But you don't know the whole story." She looks away.

"Can you tell me?"

"Can I trust you?"

"Your program helped me find the courage to be a baker and a banker. To be my independent self and be in a relationship. You can be scared and you can trust me. It can be both."

The edges of Hazel's lips move toward a smile.

"You're a smart, strong, courageous, and drop-dead gorgeous woman. You have so much insight and I think it's because you know yourself so well. You just got stuck in a story from the past. You don't have to tell me. But you can. I'm learning to walk again. Maybe I can help you too."

"That's just it. I already had to learn to walk again." Hazel sits down on the couch and holds her head in her hands.

CHAPTER 22
PROMISES PROMISES
HAZEL

"What is the real reason you're afraid?" Maxwell asks, his eyes not wavering from mine. He gently squeezes my hand.

Metal crashes against metal. Tears spring to my eyes. I'm free falling. There is no net. No safety from this crash.

"As I said, I'm afraid because my father cheated on my mom." I'm shaking and tears quietly flow from the corners of my eyes.

"Hazel, like I said, I would never do that to you."

My chest rises and falls with a deep breath. "When I was nine, my family and I were driving home from a fancy party. I sat in the backseat. It was a snowy, magical night. Or so I thought. The snow sparkled as it dusted the windows of the car. As the storm got worse, my parents' conversation in the front seat got more intense."

"I'm so sorry you had to drive back from Vermont." Maxwell's eyebrows crowd each other as he learns the source of my nerves.

I nod. "I am too but not entirely. What you were saying before about me being strong? Well, I proved that I could do a difficult thing—probably my second biggest fear. My first being you." I say that part lightly.

"When it comes to you and me, I don't want you to be afraid."

"Back to that night. The gist of their fight was while at the party, my father flirted with one of his former flings. Understandably, my mom wasn't happy about that. They hurled words like *unfaithful* and *temptation* between them. The snow turned to icy rain and pelted the windshield. Their bickering continued. '*I didn't intend to upset you. I didn't mean anything by it. Why can't you just get over it? It's not like those women mean anything.*' It took me a long time to understand that last one."

"Do you think he was still cheating?"

I nod. "Maybe? Probably? I'd like to think otherwise. The tires slipped. My father demanded to know why it mattered. It was in the past. My mother was crying by then. The arguing escalated. Then the car slid. The streetlights glinted through the glass. My parents went silent. I remained quiet. The car spun and then we were weightless before I screamed."

Maxwell's arms are around me so quickly, it's like he's bracing me, holding me fast, not letting me fall.

And for once, I don't. I remain in his arms. Holding him tightly. I sniffle a few more tears, but then they stop.

"I am so sorry, Hazel," he whispers.

"That was the last thing I remembered aside from my mother saying, "*Please don't do it again.*" He didn't answer. Was there an apology on his lips? Doubtful. I hated him for dying because I'll never know. I'll never know if he was remorseful or if he truly loved her."

Still safe inside Maxwell's hug, the drumming under his ribs is a steady, assuring beat. It tells me what my father couldn't tell my mother. Maxwell cares. He truly cares.

Still clutching me close he says, "If you'll consider being with me, I'll always talk to you about us. For instance, I'll admit it's my fault when I forget to pick up the dry cleaning. I'm also rubbish at putting down the toilet seat. I do take out the trash, put the cap on the toothpaste, and prepare the coffee maker the night before. As it turns out, I'm also a great baker. But I have flaws too."

I snort a little laugh.

"If we fight, I'll try hard to remember it's about an issue we have and not take cheap, potshots. My mother was the queen at telling my father that he'd become a fat cat, emphasis on fat when they'd argue about money. No offense, Mew," Maxwell calls in case the cat can hear through the wall. "I will always hug you when you need a hug, hold you tight when you're sad, give you space when you need to breathe. I'll put you before work and technology and distractions. And I will never, ever cheat on you." The last he says with such forcefulness, I sit up straighter.

"Can you really keep that promise?"

"On my life and every cookie I've ever baked."

It's hard to picture him in a relationship, but because he and I were so much alike, I'd imagine he'd be the one doing the heart breaking. Not the other way around. The story about his college girlfriend makes me stew.

He bites his lip then says, "Back in college, I'd even been looking at engagement rings. I thought about how I was going to ask her parents. I had dreams for the future. And it all came crashing down. But I realize now, as awful as that was, it was a warm-up. A way to teach me how fragile hearts are and how to handle them with care. To know what to look for in engagement rings and how to approach parents..." Maxwell wears a funny smile. Even after all this time, looking at the past isn't easy.

We hug and kiss and comfort each other. We assure each other. We decide to go on a date. I'll wear my new high heels and take it from there. Then…

Then I poot. It's not-quite silent. Certainly not like Polly Spoonwell. But all the same, it's a horrible sound and my cheeks go red and I dive under the couch pillows.

Maxwell doesn't run off or tease me. Instead, he goes after

me, fingers tickling under my arms and behind my knees. I giggle, writhe, and laugh some more. Thankfully, I don't pass gas again.

It had been brewing for a while. I blame it on the hardboiled egg I had with lunch. It was the kind of poot that sneaks up unexpectedly. That just demands release without any warning. Don't even pretend as if you don't know what I mean. Now, I'm humiliated. A burning, hot flush runs from my mascara-streaked cheeks, across my chest, right into the deepest depths of my ego.

I wiggle away, crawling toward the door.

Maxwell goes still. He wears a neutral mask. Switzerland embodied. No judgment. No conflict. An architect's dream of planes and intersecting lines and intrigue. I try to hold it in, I do, but then the laughter returns. Long and loud. Louder than the poot. Mrs. Hess down the hall is going to complain.

Maxwell joins me and we laugh so hard I start crying again. In a relationship, I suppose there's nothing wrong with getting a little silly too.

We talk about the episode of Friends with the fart.

We laugh until our bellies ache.

Eventually, I return to my apartment with my own promise. I'm going to get honest with myself and figure out if we can move forward. I already know my answer but have to convince that stubborn voice in my head.

I curl up with Mew and think about what it's going to take to make us work: courage, clarity—me really thinking about my wants and desires.

I'll have to clean my dishes and not nitpick about the laundry ending up next to the basket instead of inside it. I might even have to poot in front of Maxwell from time to time. Like every twenty years, if we're lucky enough to last that long. No pressure or anything.

I bury my head in my hands. Seriously, who have I become? Mew nudges his head against my hand. I scratch behind his ears and then stroke his back until he's purring.

I told Maxwell everything. I laid my fears bare. I pooted in front of him. It wasn't so bad, but it was also the worst. What am I going to do? Come home, alone, to Mew for the rest of my life? Run from date to date? From demons of the past that I've allowed to ruin the present? From true emotional intimacy?

If that's all there is, I don't want it.

I want something real. Even the pooty parts.

I call Catherine. With the time difference, she should be well into Sunday brunch over there in Italy. When she answers, her voice is cheerful. Traffic and tourists jibber in the background.

"I ordered the same kind of coffee at least three days in a row. I've lost track. Vanilla lattes."

She's quiet a moment as though trying to make sure it's me on the other end of the line.

"Does this have anything to do with Maxwell?"

"Yes."

"Did he give you *the look*?"

"The one that melted my heart or the one that says *in a room full of women and other distractions, I only have eyes for you*? If so, both. Passion and intimacy in the eyes. Full on, tractor beams, drawing me in hook, line, and sinker."

"I had a feeling. I've been making wishes in fountains all over this country. Love is in the air."

"Though we haven't been in a room full of beautiful women unless you count Lottie, Colette, and Minnie."

"All beautiful. All women."

"But I'm a mess."

"What else is new?" By the lightness in her voice, I can practically see Catherine's smile, bright under the Italian sun.

"I'm a blubbering, crying, laughing, I-don't-know-what-ing mess."

She laughs. "If you recall just a few months ago I was feeling much like you. Now I'm happier than ever."

"So it's going well with Kellan?" I interject.

She answers with a brief digression about romantic Rome,

Kellan, and how mad they are for each other. Then she says, "Why are you resisting? Is he secretly married? A criminal? Wait, is it because he was part of the Valentine's Day Date Double Dare?"

"No. It goes further into the past than that."

"Do you want me to make a pros/cons list for you?" Catherine is big into lists.

"That could take a while and..." My body hums electric, a magnetic pull drawing me toward the wall Maxwell and I share.

"How about the abbreviated version? Is your excitement to see him overwhelming? Do you visualize a future with him in it? Do you feel distracted and can't stop thinking about him? Do you feel giddy? Fuzzy inside? Swoony?"

"Mushy. Very mushy. As for the rest? Check and check and check. But also afraid and cautious and like I'm fighting an inner battle with the woman I've been for a decade."

"What's the worst that could happen?" Catherine asks, exasperated.

"I could turn out like my father."

"You've already broke that mold."

"How so?"

"You're one of the most honest people I know. Sometimes to a fault."

"I could turn out like my mother."

"Nope. You're on your own journey. And if one of you ends up with a broken heart, the great thing is that means you got to experience love. And you don't have to worry; I'd be there for you in a minute...with cookies."

"About that..." I tell her about Maxwell's passion for baking.

"Looks like you found yourself a keeper. I tell you, my grandmother's cookie recipe is magic."

"But what about him? What if I break his heart?"

"I'm not even going to answer that because you don't have to play the worst-case scenario game. It's not a productive use of your time."

"But I've been doing that my whole life, jumping from success to success because I'm afraid I'll fall."

"Hazel Loves, if you fall, you'll get right back up. Well, after eating some of this chocolate I picked up at an adorable little market. I promise. And if for some reason you can't find your footing—in this hypothetical scenario—, I'd help you. So would Lottie and Colette, all of us."

It's true. They would. But I realize something else. If I fell, I'd be able to pick myself up. After all, I am Professor Loves-Her-Life.

"Okay." I stride to the door.

"Okay?" she asks as though convincing me was easier than she expected.

"Yes." I turn the knob.

"You're going to see him now?" she asks knowingly.

"Yes. I'll talk to you soon," I whisper and leave the phone on the little table under the buzzer by the door.

Maxwell is waiting in his doorway as if expecting me. "Hazel, I want to be your Sunday morning, not just your Saturday night."

Like in a movie or one of Catherine's romance novels, I rush into his arms.

We hug and hug and hug and I realize this is a kind of intimacy too: letting him know he's wanted and that I want him even if there are risks involved.

"Wait, I have something for you," I say.

I turn back to my apartment, get a little wax bag from my jacket pocket, scoop up Mew, and close the door behind me.

I pass him the bag. "It's more than a few days old and mostly just crumbs now, but I saved the other half of my cookie for you. If you don't want to eat it you don't have to. It's more of the idea. I always want to share my cookies with you. Big ones, small ones, burned ones. Perfect ones."

His smile lights up the dim hallway. "In that case, I'd like to invite you over tomorrow for cookies."

"You know my love language."

"There's a reason for that, you know." Maxwell's lips quirk.

"And what's that?"

He brushes his thumb by my bottom lip. I shiver.

His almost-brown eyes hold mystery. A secret. "It's because I love you, Hazel."

My heart skips a beat. Because it wasn't a secret. Not at all because I knew it. My heart knew it. But I'm not sure he knows the truth of my heart.

I take a deep breath. "I love you too, Maxwell."

"Hazel Loves Maxwell. Has an interesting ring to it," he says running my first and last name with his.

"Well, it's true. The truest thing I know."

At that, we kiss in the hallway, until Mrs. Hess's door opens and closes and the dog barks.

Strange, this is exactly where we met.

CHAPTER 23
VICTORIA SPONGE CAKE
MAXWELL

My ankle is nearly healed and I'm looking forward to going back to work, hitting the gym, and sweeping Hazel off her feet.

Also, I'm looking forward to wearing regular pants instead of joggers.

Hazel is supposed to come over after she teaches her class. I could make a cake. This feels like an occasion to celebrate. My sponge cake recipe is nearly perfect. I turn up the music and get out all of the ingredients to make Catherine's grandmother's famous cookie recipe instead because it's guaranteed she'll like them.

I should probably come up with a new name for the cookies. Catherine's Grandmother's Chocolate Chip Cookie Recipe is a mouthful, especially if your mouth is full. Also, I add a sprinkle of flaked sea salt on the top, so I've officially made them my own. I have Polly Spoonwell to thank for that trick. The salt enhances the flavor of the chocolate. Also, I use dark chocolate chips because Hazel prefers them so it really amps up the cocoa content.

On the top of the piece of paper with the recipe, I cross out the title and write *Hazel Loves Cookies* then in parentheses I add

Hazel Loves me. I'll never forget the moment I told her I loved her and when she replied with the same. It was a turning point. One door closed on the past. Another opened for our future.

I scan the recipe to make sure I have everything. Catherine's grandmother's secret ingredient was cream cheese and my mouth waters anticipating taking a bite fresh from the oven.

I'm about to cream the butter, cream cheese, and sugar, when I measure it and come up short. How can I be out of sugar? I check the little bowl by the coffee maker, but it's empty.

I hobble down the hall and knock on 1G. Rabid barking pounds through the door. I call, "Mrs. Hess. Are you home?" The dogs claw at the wood. "It's Maxwell from down the hall."

I try the other guy's door, but either he's not home or can't hear me over the barking. I pass the window to the fire escape as the wind whips the icy snow off of the pane. I hope Mrs. Hess isn't out in the nasty weather—it reminds me of Hazel's story about the accident.

My stomach drops just thinking of it. I suit up, prepared to head to the market to get sugar when I hear laughter from behind Hazel's door. I didn't think she was home.

I knock. Wearing a button-down shirt that looks startlingly familiar, leggings, and her fuzzy slippers, Hazel wrings her hands.

"I thought you were teaching."

"Class was cancelled because of the weather."

From Hazel's back, a woman appears who is almost identical, but a couple of decades older.

I suddenly wish I had on my suit pants and the button-down.

"You must be Maxwell. I'm delighted to meet you. I've heard so much about you. I'm Victoria." Hazel's mother also has a British accent, but it's more refined. Also, her skin is a shade darker.

Hazel lets out what sounds like a long-held breath. "Mum, meet Maxwell. Maxwell, Mum."

We shake, but she pulls me into a European style hug with a kiss on each cheek.

"I'm only in town for a little longer, but glad I got to see my Hazel-poo."

Hazel-poo as in poot, I mouth when Victoria reaches for her coat.

My girlfriend gives me a sharp, *don't you dare* look.

I smirk. "I don't mean to bother you. I'm wondering if you can spare a cup of sugar."

"Oh, she'll gladly give you some sugar, darling. And I'm just leaving. I'm sure I'll be seeing you at the wedding."

Hazel's jaw drops.

"What?" Victoria asks. "Darling, I've never seen you like this for one. For two, you wanted to talk about my marriage to your father. That can only mean one thing."

Hazel's phone rings and she runs from the room.

Victoria smiles genially. "I've always wanted the best for my daughter and I trust you fit the bill."

"About that." I pull out the replacement ring that I've been carrying around for weeks. The other one was from a different chapter in my life. This one has a diamond and a subtle sapphire loop around the two carat stone, like her eyes. Both. "Do you think she'll like it?"

Victoria beams. "She'll love it. But it's the devotion behind it that counts. Learned that the hard way. The size of the rock doesn't matter. It's how much of a rock the man is. Steady. Faithful."

"I give you and her my word."

Victoria sucks in her cheeks like that remains to be seen, but I will prove myself to Hazel for the rest of our days.

On second thought, I should've made that sponge cake.

Hazel appears then, looking flustered and nervous.

"Everything okay?"

"I just got an offer for UUniversity. The same company who

bought my app, want to purchase the program for four times the price. Four times." She pauses. "I have to think about it."

"You two have a conversation to have and cookies to bake. I will be on my way." Victoria gives Hazel a quick kiss on each cheek and then breezes down the hall.

"Unexpected visit?" I ask.

"Sort of. I called her late last night. She was on the first plane here. Seven hours from our conversation and she was standing in my living room." A pair of tears slowly track down her cheeks. "She knew I needed her. To hear and see and know that my love story is mine. Well, ours. Yours and mine. Also, it gave her an excuse to go shopping in Manhattan. My father had a heck of a life insurance plan plus investments. Despite the heart break, she's set for life."

I give Hazel the warmest hug I can.

"I'm still shocked she came all this way."

"It's called unconditional love. Knows no bounds or borders. It's the kind I have for you."

"Even if I poot?"

"Hazel-poo?"

Her cheeks turn a soft rose and then she giggles.

I kiss her on the lips to show that I'm not put off by the occasional poot.

"What kind of sugar did you need?"

"That kind," I say around a smirk. "But granulated table sugar will do. Caster sugar is what I think you call it in the UK."

She scrounges around in the kitchen before we head back to my apartment and talk some more about Hazel's mother's visit and their conversation about her father. She says it was healing, a way to let go of the past.

"I started off mis-measuring ingredients. Burning a tray or two of cookies. Overall, getting the recipe wrong."

"Every cookie you've ever shared with me has been perfect."

"Like I said, trial and error."

"And commitment."

"Letting myself get up to my elbows in dough. In the stickiness of life." I realize we're speaking in metaphor. "That's the recipe for a successful relationship."

"And honesty, trust, communication."

"Definitely," I add. "From now on, whatever we bake, we bake together."

Hazel tilts her head from side to side. "I like it better when you bake. But how about this, I'll clean up? Wash all the bowls and pans. Team work."

I nod. "I like that. Whatever I bake and you clean up, we eat together."

She beams a smile. "Sounds like the perfect recipe."

"What your mother was saying about marriage..." I bite my lip, trying to gauge Hazel's temperature on the subject.

She covers her face with one hand. "Do you remember that first time we met in the hall with Catherine and I was going on about my wedding day?"

I smile. I'll never forget. "Is it something you want someday?"

Her eyes flash to mine. "Of course. But first, cookies."

Thirty minutes later, the apartment smells like home, and I take the tray from the oven. I pop a second batch in using the remaining dough, pour two glasses of milk, and join Hazel on the couch.

The buttery, crispy, chocolaty disc of perfection melts in my mouth when I take a bite. Just when I go for a second, I change my mind and plant my lips on Hazel's.

She grips my jaw between her hands, kisses me once, twice. Then again.

My hand brushes the bare skin on her neck. I kiss her once, twice. Then again.

"You are an exceptional baker," she breathes.

"You are an exceptional kisser," I reply.

We kiss with the hunger that food, even exceptionally delicious cookies, can't provide.

As if that weren't enough, I trail kisses behind her ear, down her neck, and across her collarbone. She laces her arms around my neck, drawing me closer. The kiss deepens, and it's as if our past fears and hang-ups drift away, dissolving in the snow as the flakes fall softly to the ground.

When we part, Hazel says, "Late in the season for a snowstorm, huh."

"Nature threw a curveball."

"What will we do if nature throws us one of those?" she asks.

"We'll bake and clean up whatever mess we make," I say with a wink.

On Monday morning, Hazel comes with me to my doctor's appointment. After an examination and another X-ray, I finally get the okay to walk without the boot.

Hazel asks questions about recovery exercises and bone alignment. Dr. Lee answers patiently even when she has him go over it again just so I don't risk re-injuring my ankle.

We both cheer when we step outside onto the bustling sidewalk. But my leg is stiff. I hesitate, and duck into the alcove of a nearby building, out of the flow of foot traffic.

"I know you want to take it slow," I say.

Her brow furrows. "I cleared my schedule for today so there's no rush...Wait, you said I want to take it slow. Remember, I was a runner in high school and college. If you want to sprint, you've met your match, buddy."

I laugh.

"I mean us. What I want to ask is if you're ready to go out on a date with me." Another question gets in line behind that one. I'm afraid I wear a bashful smile because asking a girl on a proper date isn't something I do often.

"I'd like that."

"I'll pick you up at seven."

We head back to our building, but instead of plopping back on the couch like I've been doing for weeks, I sneak back outside.

While the city comes awake from under a glistening blanket of snow, I take a long walk through Central Park. I pick up a paper cup of coffee to warm my hands as I reflect, consider, ponder, and prepare.

I watch while pigeons peck at the ground in search of breakfast. Their feathers shine opalescent under the blue sky of a winter's day. A large husky lumbers by, leading its owner through the snow.

Most of the pigeons scatter, but a few hold their ground. They're actually rather plucky birds with their understated plumage, resourcefulness, and determination. Hazel's theory about swans, peacocks, and pigeons comes to mind.

My steps are surer than ever, even over the icy ground, even after the injury. For the first time, I am certain where my future leads me and who I'm going there with. We may not be able to fly, but Hazel and I are swans, destined to be together for life.

CHAPTER 24
THE DATE OF A LIFETIME
HAZEL

I change outfits three times. Considering Maxwell has seen me in my pajamas, with bed head, and in tears, you wouldn't think it would be so difficult to pick out something to wear. At last, I settle on a champagne colored dress stitched with small beads that look like liquid gold. My earrings are long, and my hair is blown out to voluminous perfection. I feel glamorous and pretty, yet demure because this is my first official date with Maxwell Davis.

I smile at myself in the mirror when he knocks on the door. I grab the pan covered in tinfoil on the counter, my coat, and keys before giving Mew a little pat on the head.

Maxwell's eyes swallow me whole. "You look beautiful." He kisses me on the cheek.

"I made these for you." I hold out the pan.

He takes it in his hands and inhales. "I didn't know you could bake."

"Let's just see if you can clean up later." I wink. "Oh, and they're dirty brownies—dirty as in indulgent."

"Mmm, they smell delicious. And to think, I made you a batch of cookies for dessert. I hope you have an appetite tonight." He leaves the pan in his apartment and then juts out his elbow.

I take it as we walk to the elevator, looking forward to coming home later. Don't get me wrong, you know I love to eat, but dessert with Maxwell is the best.

"By the way, those shoes look perfect on you," he says.

"They were a gift from my favorite person. He's a banker and a baker..."

"And he loves you."

Maxwell kisses my cheek.

Our reflections shine in the elevator doors. "I definitely like the way you look beside me. And in front of me when we're talking to each other. And when you're deep in thought, practicing yoga—I like you all ways, Hazel Loves."

I smile and smile and smile. The night is crisp as we step outside to the waiting cab. I'm not sure exactly where we're going—well, specifically, tonight we're heading to a French restaurant on Waverly that Tyler has been raving about. But where are we going in general? All I know is that Maxwell is my destination and we're starting a new adventure right here, right now. I squeeze his hand.

"Remember when we were driving to Vermont, and we were playing that game?" he asks.

"Yeah."

"You said you'd never been in love…"

"Uh, huh," I reply. "But that's not true anymore. I'm in love now."

His smile lights up the night. After the cab lets us off, we walk toward a park, glistening under the fresh snow and in the soft lights.

I turn all mushy and emotional inside. "I told you how I felt the other day, but I'm so sure of it right now I could shout it from the rooftops. Something I never thought was possible has become, suddenly, very much a reality."

"Are you saying what I think you're saying?" I ask.

"I think I am."

"And that is…?"

"I've said it once, twice, and I'm ready to say it a thousand more times, at least. I love you, Hazel."

"I love you, more than cookies and brownies. More than anything or anyone."

We kiss and kiss.

I break away, and say, "I cannot wait to get back to his apartment to have dessert."

"We could go now," he suggests.

"What about our date?"

"Oh, right." But then he lowers to a bench, drawing me closer. "I'd get down on one knee, but given my recent injury, I should be careful."

My pulse quickens. This is not what I thought he was saying.

"Ah, heck with it." Maxwell lowers to one knee and pulls a small blue box from his pocket. "Hazel Aphrodite Loves, I love you and I want to spend the rest of my life with you. Will you marry me?"

I squeak then I squeal and then I bounce on my toes. "Yes, yes, I will."

He slides the glistening and giant ring on my finger and lifts to his feet.

"I couldn't wait a moment longer." Then he confesses he was going to ask me during the crowning glory presentation at the baking contest.

"But Polly ruined it."

"No, she just gave us a chance to sort out the past so we have a clear path into the future. It doesn't matter how long we're engaged as long as we're together."

I glimpse the ring and Maxwell's twinkling eyes. "Forever," I whisper. For the first time in my life the notion doesn't scare me. Nope. It thrills me.

He continues, slightly nervously, which is adorable. "Then I was going to ask you later, back at my place while we were eating dessert. But—"

"But I want to celebrate. I want it to be official. I want to tell the world. I want to be with you for the rest of my life." I sling my arms around his neck. I step back and admire the ring and then meet Maxwell's sparkling eyes again. "I've never wanted something with someone so much in my life."

I kiss him again and we continue to the restaurant. I can't help myself and tell everyone we encounter. We're congratulated and people ask about our plans—have we set a date, picked a location, arranged our honeymoon.

Not yet. Soon.

After we eat dinner, we head back to Maxwell's apartment. While he gets dessert, I stand by the window, looking out over the city.

The offer to buy UUniversity hangs in my mind. I created it to form community, to help people figure out a way forward. Funny, it helped me as much as I've been told it helped others.

I'm not entirely sure what comes next for me, other than a large wedding with friends and family and a honeymoon with just Maxwell and me.

Maybe I'll find my next big purpose there, a creative project that lights me up and drives my passion. Maybe not. Whatever I do, I'll keep living my dreams, trusting my man, and loving life.

Maxwell sits down on the couch and I join him.

Before I settle in for dessert, I say, "Love is strange."

"Why? You read love stories and we use it all the time: I love pizza. I love football. I love dogs. I love the Caribbean. I love—"

"I love you," I say with all the confidence in the world. "But what was that about loving dogs? Mew is going to be very upset."

Maxwell chuckles. He takes my hands. Linked, they rest on the cushion between us. My ring sparkles.

"Hazel, I wasn't looking for marriage—not to avoid family insistence because I was still single or because of my age. I wasn't seeking someone to complete me. That's way too much pressure between two people. I wasn't looking for my life to change. But the truth is, I didn't know what I was looking for until I met you."

Never mind leaving my body, my breath clears the room. I'm suspended by the feeling behind Maxwell's words.

"This isn't a crush, Hazel. It's not just that I'm infatuated with you. I can define those feelings. But this is something more. It's here." He pats his chest.

I suck in a breath. This is all the assurance I need. My fears are quelled. My worries left somewhere on the side of the road when I was nine. It's like a shroud lifts. My vision clears.

I've had three marriage proposals and two guys profess their undying love. All five were very questionable. One was at a club. Another in Bali at a yoga retreat. One was on a dance floor in Biarritz. One was during high school and the other from a man twice my age. All of them seemed uncomfortable or delusional or inexperienced.

Maxwell isn't any of those. He is my true love. My happily ever after. And I know it's true.

My heart thunders in my chest. Storm clouds gather in my brain. The part of me that was insecure and forged from the ashes of my father's trespasses flees before me. At last, I am truly free.

"I thought I was afraid of falling in love, but I'm not. Not anymore. Really, the only thing of concern is pooting in front of you."

His laughter comes from his belly. "But you already did. That ship has sailed. There's nothing you could do to diminish my attraction to you."

"Are you afraid of anything?" I ask.

"Losing you. I can't get you out of my head. I can't stop thinking about you. I want to be next to you. I don't want anything but you. Before it was about what women could do for me. Now, I want to know you intimately so I can learn what I can do for you." Maxwell lets out his breath and then continues, "Every time I look at you, I see something new and more beautiful than the last. This little part of your shoulder for instance." He kisses it. "I can hardly focus on work stuff. When your footsteps come down the hall, I get excited to hear about your class or what you did that day. I daydream about you." He smirks. "I also just want to hold your hand." He squeezes his fingers more tightly around mine. "I want to hear about your hopes and dreams and help make them happen. And I don't even care that I sound like a big fluffy marshmallow."

"Well, as you know, I'm the mushy marshmallow."

We both chuckle.

Then I go quiet. "You don't have to worry about losing me because I'm never getting lost again. The hot mess express has reached its destination. Been decommissioned. I found my way. It leads to us."

The moment flickers and sparks between us. I edge closer to him on the couch and we kiss.

When we part, Maxwell says, "Now, how about dessert?"

We each take a cookie and tap them together.

"Cheers."

"To our future," Maxwell says.

"Now, I was thinking. For the wedding cake, what would you think of a giant cookie tower?"

Once more we laugh, and whatever the future brings, I know it'll be sweet.

BOOK 3 SNEAK PEEK

Check out book 3 in the series. An Accidental Love Story with the blurb and then chapter 1:

Girl walks into clinic to donate blood. Girl passes out. Guy comes to her rescue. Guy happens to be Cutie McCute Stuff and has a medical degree.

To say I'm accident prone is an understatement. More like unlucky in life, love, and Labradors—and I have the scar to prove it. In fact, my coworkers call me Luckless-Lottie.

Dr. Russel Koenig is out of my league, off-limits. Not an option. End of story.

Only, through a cruel twist of my bad luck, the good (looking) doctor purchases his ailing grandmother a dog—the kind my parents breed. They want me to work as the liaison even though I limped away from the family business long ago.

When Russel's Oma mistakes me for his girlfriend, he doesn't correct her. Maybe my luck has changed. Our first kiss certainly doesn't seem like CPR practice.

Is my latest accident the beginning of a new chapter, prompting me to step out of my comfort zone and pushing me right to the edge of what I thought I was capable of, or will rotten luck reign, leaving me forever lonely?

Chapter 1: Missteps and Misfortune

Lottie

Confession: I don't love dogs. I don't even like them. They're drooly and smelly and dangerous, for starters. Also, they lead handsome men around by their leashes, and into picnic areas where innocent women like me sun themselves on the first real day of spring.

A grassy patch of real estate in Central Park on this fine April day was hard to come by, but I managed to secure one with an old sheet folded in half, anchored by a picnic basket, my bag, and shoes on each corner, and enough room for Minnie and a bowl of cherries between us. Cherries and Cheetos. Priorities, people.

A dog, leading a hipster wearing a pair of cut-off shorts and a Fedora, approaches, sniffling, snuffling, and nosing its way toward my snacks...and my *business*. You know, how dogs do.

Before I can get a good look at the guy, I leap back, scattering the Cheetos. "Oh no, you don't!"

Minnie yelps. "What is it?"

I point to the Australian Shepard with light brown patches as it hoovers our snacks.

Then, all of a sudden, my vision narrows. I squeeze my eyes shut. *Please, not now.*

I enter what feels like a tunnel that gets smaller and smaller no matter how much breathing I do.

No.

The dewy grass itches my ankles and sweat dots my hairline. My mind races with anxious thoughts: dog, teeth, the attack.

No, no, no.

The world tilts and gravity gives way. I reach out for something to hold onto, peering out from under my sunhat at a pair of dark brown eyes gazing at me with concern. I wouldn't say no to a cute guy gallantly stepping in to break my fall. But no. He shuffles backward.

Actually, the look I get is more like pity as an unpleasant odor wafts under my nose.

Hold on. Is he eyeing me with disgust?

Then I realize what happened. Not only was the dog nosing its way toward my no-no square, the dog-nose no-fly zone, the animal relieved itself in the middle of the picnic area, and in my moment of anxiety, I stepped in it.

Can I disappear now? Please? Pretty please with a cherry on top? At least time freezes for a second. Well, not really, but it sure feels that way as people slowly turn to watch, in their aloof New Yorker way, what transpired.

Phones come out. I'll be a meme in less than sixty seconds.

My real confession is that dogs terrify me and instead of behaving like a normal human, I lurched away, froze, and then stepped in a turd.

However, it should come as no surprise. Not to me. Not to Minnie. Maybe to Mr. Fedora.

"Oh, um." I give my foot a shake, trying to discretely wipe the poo off my strappy sandal and praying it doesn't come into contact with my foot.

The guy tucks his hand into a bag, picks up what remains of the dog droppings, and then with a tip of his cap saunters off.

"A tip of his cap? He fancies himself a gentleman after that complete disregard for my—?" I shake my head slowly.

Minnie's mouth opens and closes like she wants to say something.

"And that mongrel ate our Cheetos," I mutter, leaving out the obvious. Namely that Mr. Fedora let his dog use our picnic area as its toilet, had no discretion when it snuffled me while I was lying on the ground reading, allowed it to eat our snacks, and then didn't offer to help me clean his dog's poo off my sandal. I mean, seriously?

"And you have chicken legs," I shout to the guy—not the dog—even though he can't hear me.

"Exactly what I was thinking," Minnie says, handing me a wet wipe and hand sanitizer.

"Thanks. You're a lifesaver."

"Were you alright back there? You looked a little—" Her brow furrows.

I do my best to clean my sandal and the mess from our snacks. "Yeah. Oh. That. Um. Yeah. You know. I'm not a huge fan of four-legged fellows."

"Or the two-legged kind. That guy was a turd. Cute, but a turd nonetheless." Minnie suppresses a smile.

"Exactly what I was thinking," I echo.

Please don't hate me. My best friend Catherine is a dog freak, and she still invites me out to meet for coffee and over for a girls' nights in despite our differences. I have no doubt she and her husband will have, like, ten kids, but in the meantime, she's rescued at least a dozen dogs and counting.

The general dislike for dogs goes back to my childhood and a time I'd rather not think about.

Minnie puts on her shoes. "I hate to break up the party, but my lunch break is over. Tess will string me up if I'm not back to string up the Easter garlands."

"I'll have to stop by McKinney's and have my photo taken with the Easter bunny."

Minnie's nostrils flare and her arms fold in front of her chest. "Actually, it's the Easter Hen this year."

"Don't tell me Briony had something to do with that."

"She's firm on the fact that rabbits don't lay Easter eggs. Obviously, but when has that ever mattered before?"

"At least you don't have to deal with the soft boiled egg and his spider knuckled sidekick."

"Are they still giving you a hard time?"

"In their subtle, backhanded, evil way? Yes. Well, probably. I wasn't sure if the department-wide email from my account asking for donations to a Go-Fund-Me for a new gaming console was their doing or a genuine mistake."

"You have to find a new job."

"Tell me about it. Is McKinney's hiring?" I ask.

"That would be out of the frying pan and into the fire. A lateral move. Trust me, you don't want to deal with Tess and her sidekick."

We both laugh nervously, but secure employment in Manhattan isn't something to meddle with. At the moment, we both have jobs. At least for me, upsetting my coworkers and worse, my boss would be like playing with fire. The kind of fire that gets a person *fired* and could land me back in Wisconsin, or worse, homeless.

In ten minutes, I'm back in my cubicle at Mount Sinai. My thankless job is in the medical billing department. For such a prestigious hospital, concerned with health, you'd think there'd at least be a window. Instead, I get to stare at a cement wall.

Or, in this instance, because I was fifty-four seconds late, I come up against the brick wall that is my boss, Jim Gorham, aka the hard-boiled egg.

"Miss Sch—" He stops short of bothering to pronounce my last name.

"Schweinswald. Lottie Schweinswald."

He taps the fake Rolex he bought on Canal Street. "You know the deal. We went over this last month. Get the data from Brooks and process it before the end of the day. And your assessment is due." Gorham sweeps away but not before picking up a stack of files and unloading them into my arms, which already hold a picnic basket, my purse, and a lemonade.

I struggle to balance it all while Brooks adds to my load. "The data."

You'd also think in a modern facility like this, there would be less paper. Alas, I'm the sorry sucker who has to transcribe medical data from the doctors and departments that do things old school and then apply billing codes. *What is my life?*

"What's that smell?" Brooks sniffs the air and frowns.

That would be my dignity in the dumpster, sir.

Instead, I say, "It's a beautiful spring day. If there were a window, I'd open it and let in the fresh air." *And throw you out of it.* I offer a broad smile.

Before you think I'm a violent jerk, at least let me approach the bench and defend myself.

Between Gorham and Brooks, they've nicknamed me:

Porklip (because I have a large upper lip, I guess)

Batwoman (I had a bat in the cave, aka a booger in my nose during a meeting. Someone could've told me)

Starbucks (hey, caffeine is a necessary vitamin, mineral, and vegetable)

Montana (which I figured out was a reference to the movie Scarface. That's just cruel)

Unlucky Lottie (because it's a fact)

Then with the click, click, click of high heels, Monica Wanamaker struts in.

Of all the days.

I'm seated in the back corner, tucked into my cubicle when the woman with impossibly silky hair and the top two buttons of her shirt open smiles smugly at all us sorry suckers in billing. She smooths the piece of paper on her clipboard and poises the pen smartly. The staff and half the doctors adore her, along with her legion of minions. If Mount Sinai were a high school, she'd be the queen bee of the popular crowd. In fiction, her group would be called the *Pretty Committee*, the *Chic Clique*, or something equally inane. It isn't that I'm jealous or angry, but more like I sometimes wish I were in a book. At least then, I could count on a happily ever after.

That crew has never invited me for lunch or their weekly after-work happy hours—even though they did invite Marcella, who was hired at the same time as me but in medical records. Granted, I have my group of friends from college, but it would be nice to fit in for once.

See, when all the girls were getting curves, I was getting taller, bonier—all edges and elbows. When they were wearing shorter skirts and glossier lips, I was trying to shrink myself into t-shirts with cupcakes and jeans that didn't quite reach my ankles. It wasn't that my parents couldn't afford different clothes, they just didn't notice. When I look in the mirror now, I'm finally catching up, barely. And the scar on my left cheekbone that melts into the hollow of my smile doesn't do me any favors either.

"I am here to schedule your assessments," Monica calls.

The line forms to sign up and I reluctantly budge my way into it, shuffled and jostled as everyone hurries, for no reason I can discern, to get to the front. Oh yeah, an audience with her royal majesty, Monica.

The back of my sandal peels from my heel. I mutter an,

"Ow," and slowly turn around. Emery Rogers shrugs. "Sorry, Swine."

My cheeks tinge the color of his insult. In fact, I don't have to wear rouge now because of the way everyone erupted into laughter when Gorham slaughtered my last name, Schweinswald, on that first day, earning me the nickname, Swine—among others.

Brooks snickers. Someone makes piggy noises.

Yes, I've gone to HR. No, it hasn't helped. See, the thing is, these guys are like a fraternity and all go by their last names, meet up at sports bars after work, and regale each other with stories of their exploits. *Gag.* They've worked here much longer than me, earning them a superficial sense of superiority and actual seniority.

When I was hired, they realized they could slough off their work to me and get away with checking on their fantasy football stats all day. Also, Tim Gorham is the head of HR. Yes, he and Jim are related.

"So are you Swedish or something? I once dated a Swedish girl." Rogers waggles his eyebrows.

My cheeks grow warmer as I pat the milkmaid-style braids I've been wearing since forever. It's just an easy way to style my long hair and keep it out of my face. It's kind of my thing.

Rogers says, "Are you an idiot? Did you pay attention to geography at all? Are you even alive?"

Then, like three sixth-graders, they playfully bat back and forth at each other until Monica says, "Boys."

The "boys" giggle. Seriously.

They're more like man-children.

I schedule my meeting with Monica for the next day and return to my desk. The lines on the files blur for a moment before I wipe my eyes and get to work.

It's stupid to care. I've tried to include myself, but it's like I'm invisible. Despite my ready smile, my almost-straight teeth, and improved clothes—since grade school—they don't see me. Neither did Mr. Fedora. Nor do any guys anywhere.

Am I too different? Too quiet? Too foreign?

Oh, right, the long crescent-shaped scar. That usually turns men away.

Catherine, Hazel, Minnie, and Colette have tried setting me up on dates, but inevitably my bad luck runs amok and we end up stuck in an elevator (it's not as romantic as you'd think), covered in seagull poo (some say it's good luck, I vehemently disagree), or he spots someone without a scar on her face across the room and they end up getting married (true story).

However, if I really think about what I want out of my happily ever after, I'd rather not make friends with people who're rude and who miss the little details in life because they're too loud, too afraid of humility, and their own inner quiet to actually look and listen. I'm fine being me, most of the time.

A few hours later, when chairs roll across the floor, bags zip, and computers power down, signaling the end of the day, I prepare to wander, alone, back into the beginning of spring.

Instead, Gorham strides by, "Don't forget to donate blood—you signed up."

Oh, right. That.

The charitable and arguably civic quarterly task I intentionally try not to think about. Maybe you let me off the hook about the not-liking-dogs thing. If so, thank you. But this, I know. I know. I should already be in line. It's very important. But it's also related to the dog thing.

Let's just say I'm squeamish around blood and leave it at that. No sense in digging up the past.

Drawing a deep breath, I venture out of my department, down the hall that smells increasingly like *hospital* the closer I get to the ER, and then down several more maze-like halls to the blood draw donation station.

My stomach instantly clenches at the sight of a woman

leaving with a piece of cotton and tape affixed to her arm. What feels like melting ice drops through my limbs.

No, please. Not again.

I'm hardly even in the room. I haven't given my name. As of now, there's no sign of a needle or blood. I can do this.

But here it is. There's no stopping it. The anxiety comes at me hard and fast, making everything inside weak and wobbly. The cherries and Cheetos were a bad combination. My throat tightens. I clench my jaw as my breath becomes shallow.

I reach for the doorframe at the same time as someone steps behind me. I crane my head, my vision blurring at parallel lines of concern run across a man's forehead.

His eyes are icy blue and beautiful.

Then everything goes black.

Keep Reading

BONUS RECIPE

Hazel Loves Cookies

~~Catherine's Grandmother's Famous Cookies~~

Prep Time:15 minutes

Cook Time: 8 minutes

Total time: 3+ hours, for dough chilling

Servings: about 24 cookies

Ingredients:

1 stick unsalted butter, softened

1/4 cup cream cheese (softened avoid fat-free, light, or whipped cream cheese)

3/4 cup light brown sugar

1/4 cup granulated sugar

1 large egg

2 teaspoons vanilla extract

2 1/4 cups all-purpose flour

2 teaspoons cornstarch

1 teaspoon baking soda

1/4 teaspoon salt

1 package dark chocolate chips and/or chunks
A sprinkle of flaked sea salt for finishing

Method:

1. Combine the butter, cream cheese, brown sugar, granulated sugar, egg, and vanilla. Beat on medium-high speed or mix by hand until light and fluffy. Be sure to scrape down the sides of the bowl to get it all mixed.

2. In a separate bowl, combine flour, cornstarch, baking soda, and salt.

3. Mix wet and dry ingredients together and then add the chocolate chips.

4. Scoop dough into generous tablespoon-sized balls and sprinkle with flaked sea salt. Place on cookie sheet lined with parchment paper and refrigerate for at least 2 hours or overnight before baking. Maxwell will assure you that this step is crucial!

5. Preheat oven to 350F. Bake for 8 minutes, or until edges have set and tops are pale and glossy. Don't bake longer than 10 minutes as cookies will firm up as they cool. Allow cookies to cool.

Eat and fall in love!

ALSO BY ELLIE HALL

All books are clean and wholesome, Christian faith-friendly and without mature content but filled with swoony kisses and happily ever afters. Books are listed under series in recommended reading order.

-select titles available in audiobook, paperback, hardcover, and large print-

The Only Us Sweet Billionaire Series

Only a Date with a Billionaire (Book 1)

Only a Kiss with a Billionaire (Book 2)

Only a Night with a Billionaire (Book 3)

Only Forever with a Billionaire (Book 4)

Only Love with a Billionaire (Book 5)

Only Christmas with a Billionaire (Bonus novella!)

Only New Year with a Billionaire (Bonus novella!)

The Only Us Sweet Billionaire series box set (books 2-5) + a bonus scene!

Hawkins Family Small Town Romance Series

Second Chance in Hawk Ridge Hollow (Book 1)

Finding Forever in Hawk Ridge Hollow (Book 2)

Coming Home to Hawk Ridge (Book 3)

Falling in Love in Hawk Ridge Hollow (Book 4)

Christmas in Hawk Ridge Hollow (Book 5)

The Hawk Ridge Hollow Series Complete Collection Box Set (books 1-5)

The Blue Bay Beach Reads Romance Series

Summer with a Marine (Book 1)

Summer with a Rock Star (Book 2)

Summer with a Billionaire (Book 3)

Summer with the Cowboy (Book 4)

Summer with the Carpenter (Book 5)

Summer with the Doctor (Book 6)

Books 1-3 Box Set

Books 4-6 Box Set

Ritchie Ranch Clean Cowboy Romance Series

Rustling the Cowboy's Heart (Book 1)

Lassoing the Cowboy's Heart (Book 2)

Trusting the Cowboy's Heart (Book 3)

Kissing the Christmas Cowboy (Book 4)

Loving the Cowboy's Heart (Book 5)

Wrangling the Cowboy's Heart (Book 6)

Charming the Cowboy's Heart (Book 7)

Saving the Cowboy's Heart (Book 8)

Ritchie Ranch Romance Books 1-4 Box Set

Falling into Happily Ever After Rom Com

An Unwanted Love Story

An Unexpected Love Story

An Unlikely Love Story

An Accidental Love Story

An Impossible Love Story

An Unconventional Christmas Love Story

Forever Marriage Match Romantic Comedy Series

Dare to Love My Grumpy Boss

Dare to Love the Guy Next Door

Dare to Love My Fake Husband

Dare to Love the Guy I Hate

Dare to Love My Best Friend

Home Sweet Home Series

Mr. and Mrs. Fix It Find Love

Designing Happily Ever After

The DIY Kissing Project

The True Romance Renovation: Christmas Edition

Extreme Heart Makeover

Building What's Meant to Be

The Costa Brothers Cozy Christmas Comfort Romance Series

Tommy & Merry and the 12 Days of Christmas

Bruno & Gloria and the 5 Golden Rings

Luca & Ivy and the 4 Calling Birds

Gio & Joy and the 3 French Hens

Paulo & Noella and the 2 Turtle Doves

Nico & Hope and the Partridge in the Pear Tree

The Love List Series

The Swoon List

The Not Love List

The Crush List

The Kiss List

The Naughty or Nice List

Love, Laughs & Mystery in Coco Key

Clean romantic comedy, family secrets, and treasure

The Romance Situation

The Romance Fiasco

The Romance Game

The Romance Gambit

The Christmas Romance Wish

On the Hunt for Love

Sweet, Small Town & Southern

The Grump & the Girl Next Door

The Bitter Heir & the Beauty

The Secret Son & the Sweetheart

The Ex-Best Friend & the Fake Fiancee

The Best Friend's Brother & the Brain

Visit www.elliehallauthor.com or your favorite retailer for more.

If you love my books, please leave a review on your favorite retailer's website! Thank you! xox

ABOUT THE AUTHOR

Ellie Hall is a USA Today bestselling author. If only that meant she could wear a tiara and get away with it ;) She loves puppies, books, and the ocean. Writing sweet romance with lots of firsts and fizzy feels brings her joy. Oh, and chocolate chip cookies are her fave.

Ellie believes in dreaming big, working hard, and lazy Sunday afternoons spent with her family and dog in gratitude for God's grace.

Let's Connect

Do you love sweet, swoony romance?
Stories with happy endings?
Falling in love?

Please subscribe to my newsletter to receive updates about my latest books, exclusive extras, deals, and other fun and sparkly things, including a FREE eBook, the *Second Chance Sunset*! Sign up here: www.elliehall.com ♥

facebook.com/elliehallauthor
instagram.com/elliehallauthor
bookbub.com/authors/ellie-hall

ACKNOWLEDGEMENTS

A big, heaping spoonful of gratitude to all of you who support writers, especially readers and reviewers. Thank you!

Printed in Great Britain
by Amazon